PROWLERS

DI HERO NELSON #7

M A COMLEY

ACKNOWLEDGMENTS

Thank you as always to my rock, my mother, Jean, I'd be lost without you in my life.

Special thanks as always go to @studioenp for their superb cover design expertise.

My heartfelt thanks go to my wonderful editor Emmy, my proofreaders Joseph and Jacqueline for spotting all the lingering nits.

Thank you also to my amazing ARC group who help to keep me sane during this process.

To Mary, gone, but never forgotten. I hope you found the peace you were searching for my dear friend.

ALSO BY M A COMLEY

Unfair Justice (a 10,000 word short story)

Irrational Justice (a 10,000 word short story)

Seeking Justice (a 15,000 word novella)

Caring For Justice (a 24,000 word novella)

Savage Justice (a 17,000 word novella Featuring THE UNICORN)

Flawed Justice (a 17,000 word novella)

Gone In Seconds (Justice Again series #1)

Ultimate Dilemma (Justice Again series #2)

Shot of Silence (Justice Again #3)

Taste of Fury (Justice Again #4)

Clever Deception (co-written by Linda S Prather)

Tragic Deception (co-written by Linda S Prather)

Sinful Deception (co-written by Linda S Prather)

Forever Watching You (DI Miranda Carr thriller)

Wrong Place (DI Sally Parker thriller #1)

No Hiding Place (DI Sally Parker thriller #2)

Cold Case (DI Sally Parker thriller#3)

Deadly Encounter (DI Sally Parker thriller #4)

Lost Innocence (DI Sally Parker thriller #5)

Goodbye, My Precious Child (DI Sally Parker #6)

Web of Deceit (DI Sally Parker Novella with Tara Lyons)

The Missing Children (DI Kayli Bright #1)

Killer On The Run (DI Kayli Bright #2)

Hidden Agenda (DI Kayli Bright #3)

Murderous Betrayal (Kayli Bright #4)

Dying Breath (Kayli Bright #5)

Taken (Kayli Bright #6 coming March 2020)

The Hostage Takers (DI Kayli Bright Novella)

No Right to Kill (DI Sara Ramsey #1)

Killer Blow (DI Sara Ramsey #2)

The Dead Can't Speak (DI Sara Ramsey #3)

Deluded (DI Sara Ramsey #4)

The Murder Pact (DI Sara Ramsey #5)

Twisted Revenge (DI Sara Ramsey #6)

The Lies She Told (DI Sara Ramsey #7)

For The Love Of… (DI Sara Ramsey #8)

Run For Your Life (DI Sara Ramsey #9)

Cold Mercy (DI Sara Ramsey #10)

Sign of Evil (DI Sara Ramsey #11)

Indefensible (DI Sara Ramsey #12)

Locked Away (DI Sara Ramsey #13 coming August 2021)

I Know The Truth (A psychological thriller)

She's Gone (A psychological thriller - coming September 2021)

The Caller (co-written with Tara Lyons)

Evil In Disguise – a novel based on True events

Deadly Act (Hero series novella)

Torn Apart (Hero series #1)

End Result (Hero series #2)

In Plain Sight (Hero Series #3)

Double Jeopardy (Hero Series #4)

Criminal Actions (Hero Series #5)

Regrets Mean Nothing (Hero #6)

Prowlers (Hero #7)

Sole Intention (Intention series #1)

Grave Intention (Intention series #2)

Devious Intention (Intention #3)

Merry Widow (A Lorne Simpkins short story)

It's A Dog's Life (A Lorne Simpkins short story)

Carmel Cove Cozy Mystery Series

Murder at the Wedding

Murder at the Hotel

Murder by the Sea

Wellington Cozy Mystery Series

Death on the Coast

Death by Association

A Time To Heal (A Sweet Romance)

A Time For Change (A Sweet Romance)

High Spirits

The Temptation series (Romantic Suspense/New Adult Novellas)

Past Temptation

Lost Temptation

PROLOGUE

*S*he checked herself over in the mirror for the final time, admiring her ample curves from the side. It had been a while since she'd had a date and she was worried about making the right impression. *Is my skirt too short? My blouse too tight? What if he likes his women slimmer than me? What will I do then? I knew I should have kept up my trips to the slimming club. Losing three stone was a great achievement, but I still look fat. Another couple of stone and I'd be standing here a size ten. Why hadn't I continued? Still, there's nothing I can do about that now, is there?*

Suzanna slipped on her thin jacket. Although the weather had been hot all day, it was July after all, the evenings still had a slight nip in the air. Global warming had a lot to answer for. This year in particular, it had been all over the place. Anyway, the jacket would help disguise her curves and extra layers a little, at least, that was the plan. With one last appraisal in the full-length mirror in the hallway, she smiled and nodded at the result, finally happy, and then placed her feet in the four-inch black patent stilettos, which she hoped would help slim down her legs.

All done, she left her two-bedroom house and began the reasonably long walk into town where she was due to meet her date. *Stingy cow! I should have ordered a taxi instead. I'm going to have blisters the size of Mount Everest at this rate.*

Walking down the main road, a van slowed down beside her. Suzanna kept her gaze straight ahead, not daring to look left at the occupants as it crept alongside her. She swallowed down the fear tearing at her insides. *Shit! Fuck off, weirdos!* The temperature rose in her cheeks under their scrutiny. It was a dreadful feeling, sensing you were being stared at but being too scared to do anything about it but walk on and try to ignore them. Out of the corner of her eye she saw two men up front, but she couldn't help wondering how many more were inside the van.

Jesus! Please, someone help me! Please let another car drive past and scare them off! Distracted, unable to keep her attention on walking confidently in her stilettos, she stumbled and caught her heel in a crack in the pavement. *Shit! Get a grip, girl, for fuck's sake do!* Pulling back her shoulders, exuding more confidence than she had, she set off again, hoping the van driver would get tired of taunting her and continue on his journey.

He didn't.

He stuck with her another quarter of a mile or so. Suzanna focused her gaze on the road ahead, determined to give the impression that nothing was wrong, when in reality, the opposite was true.

The driver tooted his horn once or twice to gain her attention, but her gaze remained firmly fixed on the road ahead. Eventually, she approached the junction. The closer they got to town, the heavier the traffic seemed to be getting. Relief swept through her like a tsunami of emotions.

The driver eventually gave up. He revved the engine and, with a final squeal of his tyres he darted down the next road on the right. She continued on the same route, her heart rate soon returning to near normal again after the van's exit. At one point, she debated whether to turn back, go home and give up on her date. Instead, she ploughed on. The men were probably a couple of guys out for a laugh. Some laugh that had been, they'd succeeded in scaring the shit out of her.

Suzanna changed the song in her head. This time she hummed

along to her favourite Ed Sheeran song. It did the trick, took her mind off the last ten minutes and put her back in the mood for her date. A smile fixed in place, she turned into the next street and stopped dead. There, standing across the pavement were four men. One of them was leaning against the white van which had been following her only moments earlier.

Shit! What the fuck am I supposed to do now? I can't run, not in these damn shoes! Determined not to let them see how petrified she was, she forced a smile and said, "Hello, can I help you?"

The four men, all young, laughed. She noted that two of them looked similar, as though they might have been twins. If she were to guess how old they were she'd put them between twenty-five and twenty-eight. The one with the heavily tanned face stepped away from the van and approached her. She shrank back, she couldn't help it.

"You, me and the boys here are all going to go somewhere and have a nice time."

"I'm sorry," she stuttered, "I can't. I'm on my way into town, I have a date waiting for me."

He tipped his head back and laughed. "Did you hear that, boys? She's on a date. Which means she'll be all nice and clean for us. Probably has fresh undies on, they might even be matching. Sounds like we're in for a treat tonight, eh, lads?"

Suzanna swallowed down the bile toying with her throat. "Please, no. I don't want any trouble." She scanned the area. Unfortunately, there were no houses in this part of town, only a few warehouses. *Fuck! Why hadn't I taken a taxi instead?*

Hindsight was a wonderful thing but was useless in the midst of a tense moment such as this.

"All right, let's get this show on the road. Get her in the van, guys."

Suzanna fought hard, dug her heels into several of the men's feet, but they were wearing steel-capped safety shoes, designed to ward off any sharp objects or sudden penetration. She screamed and hit out as hard as she could with her handbag and her clenched fists. But, come the end, her attempts proved pointless and the four men bundled her into the van. Once there, two men remained with her.

One on either side. She shrivelled into her shell under their intense glares.

What's going to happen to me now? What do they want from me? I hope it's not... She refused to deliberate any further, fearing it would only make the situation worse. Instead, she tried to come up with a plan, a survival plan. She was desperate enough to consider anything, even surrendering her body if it meant the men setting her free. The thought made her shudder.

The journey didn't take long. The van stopped, and the back doors were wrenched open by the two men who had been sitting up front.

"Okay, get her out. Let's get on with it. The usual place is awaiting us."

Suzanna's gaze darted around the four abductors. The two in the van beside her, turned her around and prodded her in the back to get her moving.

"All right. There's no need to push me. I'll go willingly."

"Like you have an option," one of the guys behind her muttered.

Stepping out of the van, she tottered on her heels, her legs almost giving way beneath her.

"Why do you bitches wear those things if you can't soddin' walk in them?" one of them asked.

Suzanna took it to be a rhetorical question and didn't bother answering. She followed the two men in front into the warehouse unit while the other two men walked behind her, giving her an extra shove if they thought her pace was too slow.

The group wound their way through the disused unit. Something squealed and scurried for cover off to the left. Suzanna had a sudden pain in her chest which affected her breathing. *Shit, am I having a heart attack? Maybe that would be preferable to what I believe lies ahead of me. Please, God, don't let them hurt me.*

The leader uprighted a chair in front of him, and both men behind her forced her into it. She stared up, her fearful gaze flitting between the four men holding her captive. She swallowed periodically to keep the bile at bay. At the same time, she tried to hold back the tears threatening to fall. "Please, I don't know what I've done to deserve this, please, won't you let me go?"

"Todd, Barry, you know what to do. Get her prepared," the driver said.

They handled her roughly, pulling her arms behind her back and fastening them with a cable tie. The tears slipped down her cheeks when the leader reached for the zip on his jeans. She closed her eyes, knowing exactly what was about to happen to her.

Please, God. Don't let them do this. Take me before they can kill me!

*H*ero hated receiving early morning calls from the station. He peeped at the clock—five-thirty. What a bummer! "Hello, you've reached DI Nelson's phone, he's tucked up in bed right now so this better be good."

"Sorry, sir. It's control. I think you'll want to hear this. A body has been discovered down by the River Irwell. The pathologist has requested you attend the scene."

He sat up in bed, carefully, doing his utmost not to disturb Fay. He glanced sideways and noticed one of her eyes was half-open. She groaned and rolled over. He flung the quilt back and took the call in the en suite. "Okay, you've grabbed my attention. Where are we talking about?"

"In Salford Quays, sir."

"That's a pretty big area, can you be more specific?"

"Outside the rowing club."

"Okay. I think I know the one you mean. I'll get dressed and make my way down there. Can you get DS Shaw to join me? She'll probably give you a mouthful; I'm used to her bad moods. She's not a morning person as such, as you're about to find out."

"I'll heed your warning. Thanks, sir."

He ended the call and turned on the shower, preferring to take a semi-cold one this morning to get his heart pumping faster, to ensure he was fully awake by the time he got to the scene. Ten minutes later, he'd kissed Fay goodbye and was out of the door, driving into town with Gold Radio to keep him company, along with the memories they had created as a family during the weekend.

The twins, Zoe and Zara, had started taking their first swimming lessons at the local pool. They were naturals, the coach had said. This was followed by a trip to the adventure park with Louie who was into anything with a daredevil status. He'd dashed to the top of the wall at the Manchester Climbing Centre within five minutes. Which meant he had beaten Hero by twenty minutes, the little tyke. He puffed out his chest, proud of all his kids' achievements over the weekend. He sighed, reflecting how good life was at present, after the past few years of torment they'd had to endure with the passing of his father.

Although, saying that, things were still a little fragile between his mother and sister, after his twin, Carla, found out she was pregnant after a one-night stand. Unfortunately, she lost the baby after a few weeks due to the pressure of work. Her mental state had suffered severely for a couple of months but, thankfully, she now seemed to be on the road to recovery. He and his family were making sure of that. Including her in everything they did, although she had turned down the opportunity to join them at the weekend due to being on duty at the station.

He drew up at the crime scene. Gave his name and rank to the uniformed officer in charge of the Crime Scene Log and made his way over to the pathologist. Gerrard Brown was searching for some equipment in the back of his van.

"How's it hanging, Gerrard? Got a suit for me?"

"It's hanging the same as it always does, down my right leg." Gerrard grinned and threw him a paper suit to slip into.

"Ha bloody ha. Why the right and not the left leg?"

"Personal preference. Good of you to join us so early. You didn't mind getting the shout then?"

"I did but I promise not to take it out on you. What have we got?"

"A murder scene. As gruesome as it gets, I'd say."

Hero togged up and pulled the blue plastic coverings over his shoes. He glanced up as another car appeared. His partner, DS Shaw, left her vehicle, in no great rush, spoke to the copper holding the log and ducked under the tape. Gerrard flung her a suit when she was a few feet away from them.

"Morning, Julie, lovely day," Hero said, hiding the smirk that was threatening to break free.

She grunted and mumbled, "For the damned birds maybe, not for those trying to get their eight hours in."

Hero turned away and sniggered. He cleared his throat and announced, "Let's get on with it. Lead the way, Gerrard. I'm taking it the body was dumped here, correct?"

"Yep. I think we can safely say that, just by the lack of blood around. You'll see what I mean in a moment. It's this way."

Hero looked up at the sky. Dozens of gulls circled overhead, the racket they were making painful to his ears. "Damned things. Can't stand them."

"Ignore them, they're not doing any harm," Julie muttered.

"I suppose. I bet you wouldn't be saying that if you had fish and chips in your hands."

Julie stopped walking, stared at him, shook her head and said, "Yeah, but I haven't, so what was the point in you saying that?"

Hero tutted, groaned and walked on. "What was the point indeed," he complained under his breath. His partner wasn't the easiest of people to get along with. Good at her job, there was no denying that, and while she had mellowed slightly over the years she'd been by his side, there were times, such as this, when he'd dearly love to throttle her for her lack of humour and for always seeing things in black and white. It made life boring, and there was enough dreariness to this job as it was, which was why he always tried to lighten things up now and again. Maybe that would wash with a different partner, not Julie, though. *I need to give up and stop trying. She's never going to change!*

Gerrard paused two feet from the body. Hero looked down and

sucked in a breath then let out a few expletives that earned him another backlash from Julie.

"Do you have to swear like that?"

"Sorry, inappropriate behaviour on my part. But you have to admit it's stomach-churning, DS Shaw."

"It is, I wouldn't stand here and doubt it for a second, but I still wouldn't let out some of the words you had chosen to say either," she chastised in her usual school mistress tone while not being able to take her eyes off the victim.

Hero glanced up and spotted the amused look on Gerrard's face. He glowered at him, warning the pathologist not to give his partner any more ammunition to fire at him.

Gerrard averted his eyes and pointed at the decapitated corpse. "As you can see, she clearly lost her head over something."

"Jesus! Everyone's a bloody comedian today," Julie grumbled. She took another step towards the headless victim and stared at the open wound. "No rough edges. At least it was a clean cut."

Gerrard dug Hero in the ribs. "She's good, Hero. Far more observant than you, I'd say."

"Piss off, Gerrard. I was thinking the same. I just hadn't got around to saying it, that's all. How do you think it was made? The cut, I'm talking about."

"I'm aware of what you're asking. I'll need to examine the corpse thoroughly back at the lab. However, my initial thoughts are that the injuries were performed by possibly some kind of electrical equipment."

"What? Like a chainsaw?"

Gerrard looked him in the eye and shrugged. "Unlikely, that would leave raw edges. I'll have a more definitive answer for you soon enough."

"Gee, thanks. If it does turn out to be a chainsaw, who in their right mind carries around one of those gadgets anyway? Unless their intention is to do this kind of damage to another human being."

"Exactly," Julie added. "What about a tree surgeon?"

"What about one?" Hero shot back at her.

She let out a frustrated sigh. "You just asked a question, and I gave you an answer."

"Oh right, yes, of course. Sorry, too early for me, still not functioning right."

"May I suggest you wake up quicker in that case? This is a very important investigation already."

"Ooo... get you. Okay, will do, Sergeant." He stepped closer to the corpse and crouched. Upon closer inspection he noted there was very little blood coming from the wound. He glanced up at Gerrard and said, "I see what you mean about the lack of blood. However, how sure can you be that the victim's wounds occurred pre-mortem rather than post-mortem?"

"That's why we carry out a PM," Gerrard clarified unnecessarily.

"Okay, I was only asking. Jesus, whoever did this to this woman had a severe axe to grind with her, or am I reading this all wrong?"

"I'd say you're going along the right lines with that notion. Why remove her breasts as well as her head? And not only that, her vagina has been given a different shape entirely."

"To mask any evidence, possibly?" Hero asked.

"There is that. Either way, it's sick that another human being could even consider carrying out such an attack on another. To my mind, this was a well-executed attack. I'm hoping to Christ the woman wasn't alive through most of it."

"The lack of blood backs up your comment, though, yes?"

"Not necessarily. I still believe she has been planted here, so there could be a pool of blood sitting in someone's house or vehicle right now. She could possibly have been cleaned up as opposed to cut to ribbons post-mortem."

"Either way, you're right, it is bloody gruesome and not for the faint-hearted to see at this time of the morning. All I can say is, good job I didn't have a full English inside me, it wouldn't have lasted long residing in my stomach, that's for bloody sure."

"I came to the same conclusion," Gerrard admitted beside him while Julie continued to stare at the body.

"I sense this is going to be an exceptionally difficult investigation to solve," Hero murmured more to himself than to those standing around him.

"No shit, Sherlock," Julie replied, ending her comment with an exaggerated sigh.

Hero glared at her but resisted the temptation to show his annoyance. Instead, he asked Gerrard, "Any way we're going to be able to ID her?"

Gerrard lifted one of her arms. Underneath was a tattoo, a very distinctive one. "By this, I'm presuming."

"Jesus. Is that a snake?"

Gerrard gave him one of his I-can't-believe-you-asked-me-that kind of looks. "Yes, with a human head."

Hero moved positions and peered closer at the inked skin. "Is that a name?"

"It is. Looks like *James* to me."

"James the snake or James Snake as in his surname? That's the question," Hero pondered out loud.

Neither Gerrard nor Julie replied. Hero stood up and shook out the slight cramping pins which had developed in his legs.

"All right. What about her age? Can you give me something to go on?"

"Twenties, thirties or forties perhaps. Hard to tell, no significant ageing per se, so I wouldn't say she's any older than the range I've given you."

"Good to know. It's not much but it's a start, that's all we can be thankful for at this stage, right?"

"Indeed," Gerrard admitted. "There's not a lot else I can tell you, especially with a naked body confronting us."

"Frustrating as that is, I'll get the team delving into the one clue we have got to hand, the tattoo. It's pretty distinctive, someone must know who did it. If we find that out it could lead to us identifying the poor victim."

"We could always take a picture of it and air it through the media," Julie added.

"We could, further down the line. If I were a relative of the vic, I'm not sure I'd want to hear about something like this via the media, would you?"

Julie grunted. "It was just a suggestion."

"Don't be so hard on Julie, she was only stating the obvious," Gerrard said, coming to Julie's defence.

Instead of Julie smiling appreciatively at the pathologist, she glared at him, forcing the colour to stain his cheeks. He mumbled an apology, and Hero had to turn away to suppress the giggle tickling his tonsils.

"Okay. In that case, we'll let you get on. Wait, who reported the crime?"

Gerrard jabbed a thumb over his shoulder. "Guy sitting in the car. On his way for an early morning row until he saw this and called it in. I told him to stick around, knowing that you'd want to speak to him."

"Thanks. We'll have a chat, get a statement down, and then send him on his way. Can you get the report back to me ASAP on this one? We need all the help we can get from the outset."

"You've got it. Good luck."

"I reckon we're going to need it. Thanks for getting me out of bed early by the way."

Gerrard grinned. "Always a pleasure, Hero."

Hero and Julie walked over to the car where the ashen-faced man was sitting behind the steering wheel. He stared at them as they approached his vehicle.

"He seems in shock," Julie announced out of the corner of her mouth.

"You reckon? I think I would be, too, if I'd been confronted with that corpse first thing in the morning, wouldn't you?"

"All right. There's no need for you to snap at me."

Hero cleared his throat. *Here we go, on the bloody defensive as usual. Get a life, Julie.* He chose to ignore her snide comment and tapped on the man's window. Hero produced his warrant card and showed it to the man who took his time to examine it. "We appreciate you waiting around to see us, sir. Can I ask what your name is?"

"It's Brad Cotton. I come down here regularly. A group of us do, you know, first thing, for a row, it gets the heart pumping early, sets us up for what the day has in store for us."

"And yet you're alone here. Where are the others?"

"I rang them as soon as I discovered the body. Well, after I called your lot, of course. I had a feeling the place would be swarming with coppers and told them not to bother coming down here today. The pathologist told me to stick around as you'd be needing a chat with me. So, here I am."

"Thanks, that was good of you. The less people around a crime scene, the better for the professionals involved. Is it a daily routine? You coming to the rowing club?"

"Yes, six days a week, even on my day off. Although Sunday is always spent with my family."

"As it should be." Hero smiled. Julie took out her notebook. "What time did you arrive?"

"Around four-thirty, I believe. Slightly earlier than normal as it happens."

"May I ask why?"

Brad rolled his eyes. "Pressures of work, stressed to the max, couldn't bloody sleep last night. Thought I'd show up early and do some weights in the gym before the others arrived."

"You have access to the club at all times?"

"I have a key. No one else knows that, though. The guy who runs the club is a good friend of mine. Ashley Jangles, he's called, in case you need to know."

Hero peered behind him at the buildings off to his right. "And the rowing clubhouse is which one?"

"The one on this end."

Hero squinted, cursing the fact he'd missed his latest eye examination, only because he knew his eyesight was deteriorating and he was too scared to admit he needed specs. "Ah, yes, I can see it now. We're going to need a statement from you, Brad, if you don't mind?"

"I don't. Only too willing to help, hence me hanging around to speak with you."

"Great. I wish everyone would be as considerate as you."

"My pleasure. Must be some kind of maniac with a screw loose, on the run out there, to do that sort of shit. Sickening, right? I had yoghurt for breakfast before coming out, almost brought it up when I stumbled across that."

"I take it you spotted the corpse from your vehicle?"

"I did. Caught sight of it in my headlights as I turned into the road. Found it nigh on impossible to see what it was until I got out of the car."

"Did you get close to the victim?"

"No. I kept my distance. I see enough cop shows on the TV to know how important it is to remain clear of a crime scene. Last thing I need or want is you arresting me for the damned crime." He shuddered. "I wouldn't know where to begin cutting up a body like that. It's making me gag just looking at it."

"Along with ninety-nine-point-nine percent of the population, I shouldn't wonder. Not the most pleasant discovery to make. Sorry it was something you had to deal with first thing."

Brad shrugged. "Not your fault. Still hard to fathom and to handle, all the same. Glad my usual companion wasn't here to see it, no doubt she would have fainted, giving me an added problem to solve."

"Good job indeed. Am I right in thinking you avoided the club yesterday then?"

"That's right."

Hero chewed his lip. "Are there many rowers who come down here on a Sunday?"

"Yes, loads of them. Why? No, wait, you're asking if the body was here yesterday to find out the time of death or when it might have been left here, aren't you?"

Hero smiled. "That's correct. I can tell you're well up on your procedures, sir."

"I am. I came here on Saturday, no sign of it being here then, I can tell you."

"That's useful information. Thanks. Julie, can you organise the statement for me?"

Julie's head rose from her notebook, and she nodded. "Will do. I'll get uniform to do it."

"Good. Thanks for your help, Brad. I'll leave you one of my cards. Get in touch if anything else comes to mind, if you would?"

"I'll do that. Will this area be out of action long? I need to row to balance my mental health. It suffered a lot during the lockdown, and I was just getting it back on the right track until this happened."

"Don't worry. You should be all right to use the club tomorrow. Our pathologist is efficient, one of the finest in his field."

"Excellent news. Sorry if I came across as pushy."

"You didn't. Thanks for all your help." Hero walked away, leaving Julie behind to organise the witness statement. As far as he could tell, there was only one road leading to the area. He spun around and noticed a camera over on the far side of the quay. He shook his head, aware it would be as much use as a chocolate teapot sitting in the midday sun. "Great. Nothing else obvious around here, not unless any of the shops along the quay have any form of surveillance cameras on site. Worth asking the question."

"First sign of madness, that is."

He jumped and turned round to face his partner, who had snuck up on him in her flat no-nonsense type of footwear she always chose to wear for work. "What is? And do you have to sneak up on me like that? You know how much I hate it."

"Talking to yourself, and yes, I know how much it annoys you." Julie grinned so hard her eyes crinkled up to tiny slits.

"You can be a harsh woman at times, Shaw."

"I know. I see it as my job to keep you on your toes."

He kicked out at a stone and listened to it plop over the edge of the quay and into the water.

"Sneaking up on me and you fiddling with that damned phone of yours at all hours of the day are going to drive me into an early grave, fact not fiction!"

Julie screwed her nose up at him. "I know it's early, but why do you always seem to find time to personally attack me?"

"Personally attack you? Hardly. Let's get back to the investigation before we fall out, again. I've had enough of that to last me a lifetime over the bloody years."

"There's a solution to that."

He raised an eyebrow at her. "Which is?"

"Stop having a pop at me at every given opportunity. It gets a tad tedious, just saying."

"Now you're being bloody ridiculous. Had you said that a few years ago, I would have hung my head in shame, but recently, that simply isn't true. In fact, I'd go as far as to say I believe you're talking out of your arse."

Julie inhaled a large breath then let it out, puffing her cheeks out as the air escaped her mouth. "Whatever."

"And that's another thing I hate. That stupid comeback, I'm sick to death of it."

Julie grinned and mouthed the word again then swivelled and walked away. Leaving Hero seething and grinding his teeth. *Stubborn bitch. Maybe I should ship her out, be done with it. I've been threatening to do it for years and never got around to it. Although, if I did that, I'd have to train someone else up to my way of working. Damned if I do and damned if I don't. Which is the lesser of the two evils?*

He remained studying the area for a few minutes longer and then joined his partner and Gerrard alongside the corpse. "No chance of getting any footage, not from what I can gather."

"Maybe that was the killer's intention. Why he chose this place," Julie suggested.

"He? Why does the killer have to be gender specific at this stage?" he responded sharply.

"Help me out here, Gerrard," Julie pleaded.

Gerrard laughed. "You two need your heads knocking together. You should listen to her, Hero, DS Shaw has a point. I can't see a woman having the strength to cut another person's head off, although, I must admit, nothing would surprise me these days if that turned out to be true."

Hero sighed. "Thanks for the reprimand, Gerrard."

"Ah, but if she had the right tools at her disposal, anything is possible," Julie added, never one to give in and always keen to pounce on an opportunity to prove him wrong.

"True enough. I'll give you that one, partner. Right, if you have nothing further for us, Gerrard, we'll head to the station and begin the investigation in earnest."

"I haven't. Good luck. I believe you're going to need it with this one."

"Thanks, I think you're right. Come on, Shaw, you can follow me back." He began walking towards his car and peered over his shoulder when he realised Julie wasn't following him. "Shake a leg and stop trying my patience, Shaw."

She said something to Gerrard but he was too far away from them to hear what was being said. Gerrard laughed.

"I heard that," Hero shouted, even though it was a lie.

"Wow, since when did you develop extra powers in the hearing department?" Julie swept past him and got into her car.

I'll get you for that, partner. I'd watch my back if I were you.

Julie ended up pulling out ahead of him. He followed her back to the station, deliberately driving too close to her rear bumper at times, aware how much it ticked her off. Judging by the glares she was firing his way, his ploy had worked.

When they arrived, Julie left her car and stomped through the main entrance before he'd even left his vehicle. He chuckled. He knew how childish it was to wind her up, but some days, it was worth all the angst and hissing fits just to piss her off.

He was surprised to find a cup of coffee sitting on his desk. He poked his head out of the room and said, "Thanks, I wasn't expecting that."

"I'm not as petty as you. Not that you deserve it. Can we call it quits? I'm tired of walking on eggshells around you. Worried I'll say the wrong thing at any given moment. I think we know each other well enough by now to be aware of what winds each other up. I'm tired of the games. All I want to do is come to work, be efficient and solve the crimes that fall on our desks. Is that too much to ask?"

"No, you're right. I'm sorry if I've offended you."

"You haven't. Truth is, you wear me out. Our job is tough enough as it is, without me having to keep my guard up all day long in your presence. It's tiring and stressful."

"Okay. We'll call a truce. Thanks for the coffee. I'll be dealing with the post littering my desk."

"Want me to trawl through the internet, see what I can find about the tattoo?"

"You do that."

"Then, once the parlours are open, I'll start ringing around, see if it gels with any of them."

"Brilliant." He left his partner to it and sat at his desk, the rich roasted coffee beans tantalising his nostrils. In his dreams. The vending machine coffee was passable at best. He smirked. *One lives in hope, Nelson, old boy. I'll just close my eyes when I drink it and be transported to the coffee capital of the world in my mind. It'll lessen the blow of how rancid a cup of coffee around here truly is.*

He opened the first brown envelope screaming at him on his desk and set it in the pile that would need a response later, if he got around to it. With a murder inquiry to handle, he sensed his mundane chores would soon hit the rocks and pile up, needing to be dealt with later. His mind wandered back to the crime scene. He hadn't dealt with a gruesome crime such as this in a good few years, not since the Krull Gang had plied their trade and caused untold havoc on his patch. Could this be related in some way? All the gang members were either dead or behind bars, but that didn't mean anything, he was all too aware of that. Gangs started up at the drop of a hat. He'd bear it in mind and let the rest of the team know when he held the morning briefing at just gone nine.

He took a look at his watch. It was seven-forty-five, another hour to go before the workforce joined him and his partner. He bellowed for Julie to join him.

She appeared in the doorway within seconds. "You called?"

"I did. Any luck?"

"What with?"

"You were searching the Net. the last I heard."

"Ah, yes, sorry. No luck as yet. I'll let you know, if and when I find anything. Is that all you wanted?"

"It was. Although my cup is empty and could do with topping up."

Julie collected his paper cup, peered into it and headed back towards the door. "Glad I have my uses. Use me and abuse me, why don't you?" she mumbled on her way out.

"I heard that," he called after her, laughing.

"You were supposed to," she confirmed.

He opened another couple of envelopes before she returned.

She placed the cup of steaming coffee on the desk and backed up towards the door. "Anything else you require, oh Great One?"

Hero shook his head. "I don't think so, not unless you fancy a trip out to the baker's or the café around the corner."

"You're right, I *don't*. Maybe one of the lads will go when they show up."

"I'll have gone past it by then. Never mind. There was I thinking we were getting on better and you've let me down, again."

Julie opened her mouth to complain but stopped when he burst out laughing.

"I'm winding you up. If I need to eat, I'm quite capable of fending for myself."

"Glad to hear it. I'll get back to it then."

"You and me both. Give me a shout when the others arrive. I'll plough through this lot, get it out of the way, and then we can concentrate on the investigation."

"If I ever find the bloody tattoo." Julie closed the door behind her.

Hero took a sip of his coffee and shuddered. Bitter and detestable. Why he persisted drinking it was beyond his comprehension. He went through the urgent pile and began actioning the replies. After a while, he sat back, the dreaded task completed for another day, and looked up at the grey clouds rapidly floating past his window. Another rainy day in Manchester, no doubt. *What's new there?* His thoughts lay with Cara, his twin sister, and he made a mental note to ring her later on that morning, if time permitted. At just gone nine, he joined the rest of the team who were settling into their seats, ready to start their arduous day.

"Grab yourselves a coffee, and if someone would care to buy me one, you'll be named as star copper of the week. It'll be my third cup of the day. I don't think the caffeine is doing its job, though, as I still feel half-asleep."

Jason leapt out of his seat and dealt with Hero's request swiftly and efficiently before he returned to his chair again. Hero angled the whiteboard into position and noted down the relevant facts he and Julie had obtained so far.

"So, here's the new case that dragged Julie and me out of bed early this morning."

Julie's head suddenly lifted, and she stared at him, the colour tainting her cheeks.

"Damn, I should correct what I just said, but I think it will only make matters worse. See, I told you my brain wasn't functioning properly yet. Anyhow, Julie and I showed up at the scene, in separate cars, I hasten to add, at an ungodly hour this morning, to find one of the most gruesome crimes I've probably ever encountered. The victim is a female in her twenties, thirties or forties, the pathologist was undecided. She was headless, and her breasts had been cut off."

"What the...?" Sally said with a shake of her head.

"Yep, not very pleasant, I can tell you. Given the state of the corpse, the pathologist believes that her body was dumped at the scene, due to the lack of blood in the vicinity. I don't have to tell you how difficult this case is going to be with a Jane Doe on our hands. You're going to have to dig deep, guys. Julie has already been at it for a few hours since our return. Would you like to fill the team in on what you've achieved so far, DS Shaw?"

"The truth is, frustratingly not a lot." Julie handed her phone around, showing the team the photo of the tattoo she'd been trying to track down via the internet since they'd got to the station. "This tattoo is pretty unique, I'm sure you'll agree. However, I haven't managed to track anything down over the Net yet. It's my intention to call the local tattoo parlours in the immediate area to see if they can help us out."

"I don't mind doing that, Sergeant. I have a friend who's an Inker, sorry, tattoo artist. I could run it past him and see if he can give us anything useful," Jason announced.

Julie faced Hero and asked, "What do you think, sir?"

"Hand it over. You've had enough of banging your head against the wall, I should imagine."

"True enough. Okay, Jason, I'll hand over the leads I've found so far."

"Great. I'll call my mate, Rick, after we've finished the meeting."

"Excellent, see, we're sort of making headway already." Hero grinned. "The other aspect we need to look into is that whoever dumped the body at the location, which is down at Salford Quays by the way, close to the rowing club, would have needed to have had a vehicle. I carried out a quick scan of the area and saw one CCTV camera over the other side of the quay, that's all. I'm thinking two of you should do some legwork, call at each of the shops in the area, see what footage they have and grab a copy if anything shows up. Any volunteers?"

Lance Powell reluctantly raised his arm and nodded at Sally to do the same. "Okay, the A-Team will take care of that. Jason, you pick up where Julie left off. Hopefully the information will come to us freely now the time is more respectable."

2

---

*S*everal hours later, Hero and Julie were standing in the station car park, debating whether to have some lunch or set off to the address Jason had managed to find for the victim, Suzanna Abbott. As the tattoo had been specially commissioned the body was unlikley to be anyone else. "We could pick up lunch on the way back, if we feel up to it after breaking the bad news to her family."

"That was my concern, I've already missed out on breakfast this morning."

"You're not alone there," Julie replied. Her stomach rumbled on cue, and she rubbed it.

"That settles it then. Neither of us has eaten, we'll be no good to anyone if we both pass out through lack of nutrition during the day, agreed?"

"What do you suggest?"

"We call in to the greasy spoon around the corner and order a fry-up."

"Oh, joy of joys! That place is bad artery city!"

"You needn't tag along, if it doesn't appeal to you. I need more than a sandwich, we both do."

"All right, you've convinced me. Are you paying?"

He placed a finger against his cheek and frowned. "Let me think... er, no. I have a wife and three kids to support. You're young, free and single."

"I am not. I've been living with Rob for years. We're saving up for a new house."

He just about managed to prevent himself from shuddering at the man's name. He'd never really got on with Rob, a fact Julie was totally mindful of. "Good for you. I'm still not paying. Are you telling me you can't afford four pounds fifty?"

"I can. I was counting on you showing me some sympathy."

"Ain't gonna happen, Shaw, not in my lifetime. Come on, we're wasting time." He pressed the key fob to open his car doors, and they piled in.

Hero managed to find a space in the small car park at the rear of the café. He'd rung ahead and placed the order. As soon as they'd taken their seats, the waitress appeared with a strong cup of coffee and a fried breakfast for each of them. Neither he nor Julie spoke again until they were halfway through their meal.

"Any regrets?" Hero asked.

"I'll tell you later. So, we have the woman's address. What if we get there and she lives alone?"

He shoved half a sausage in his mouth and chewed it for a while. "Then we put our detective hats on again and find her family. Maybe they've reported her missing over the weekend."

"Maybe. I suppose we should have checked that before we left the station."

"It's not too late. Why don't you give Jason a ring now?"

Julie eyed him with disgust. "Because I'm in the middle of eating my brunch."

He rolled his eyes, set his fork down on the plate and fished his phone out of his jacket pocket. Punching in a number, he waited. "Ah, just the person I wanted to speak to. Jason, do me a favour, I forgot to do it before we left the station. Can you contact Missing Persons for me, see if the victim, Suzanna Abbott, has been registered with them over the weekend?"

"On it now, boss. Any specific reason?"

"I'm wanting a next of kin address, in case Abbott lives alone at the property."

"Ah, I'm with you. Leave it with me."

Hero ended the call and scooped up a forkful of bacon and baked beans. Not long after, Jason rang back, disturbing him from eating his breakfast once again. "I knew I should have rung him after I'd finished. Jason, hi. What have you got for me? Julie, write the address down as I repeat it, would you?"

Julie looked daggers at him but extracted her notebook.

"Okay, we're ready."

"Her father notified the hotline on Sunday. She was due at her parents' for Sunday dinner but didn't show up. It's sixty-four Willow Street, Hyde, sir."

"Thanks, we'll get over there ASAP."

He ended the call and said, "Hyde to Salford Quays, what's that? About twenty minutes on a good day with very little traffic?"

Julie lifted her phone from the table and tapped in a few details. "Twenty-two minutes to be precise. See, my phone does have its uses now and again."

Hero pulled a face and tucked into the final mouthfuls of his breakfast. He washed it down with what was left of his lukewarm coffee and pushed back his chair.

"Wait, I haven't finished yet."

"I can see that. You've got as long as it takes me to have a piss to finish it."

"Charming."

His partner muttered as he left the table and darted into the loo situated on the right. Hero returned to the table to find the waitress clearing away their plates. "She's paying," he said and walked out of the café.

A livid-looking Julie emerged a few seconds later, got in the car beside him and held out her hand. "Four-fifty you owe me."

He had the change waiting for her and placed it on her flattened palm. "Your problem is?"

Hero laughed and started the engine. "Too easy, always too easy."

"What is?"

"To wind you up. Punch the address into the satnav, will you? Make yourself useful rather than just sitting there doing nothing."

Julie had the sense to ignore him. They arrived at the semi-detached house around ten minutes later to find two cars parked on the drive. One a large Merc, the other a small BMW. He and Julie approached the house. Hero hated this side of the job. In fairness, he didn't know any copper who liked it.

A woman with silver hair, wearing a matching grey suit, opened the door. "Hello, can I help?"

"Mrs Abbott?"

"Yes, that's right. I never buy from the door, but thank you for asking."

She attempted to close the door, but Hero stuck his foot in the gap.

"We're not selling anything. We're DI Nelson and DS Shaw. Would it be possible for us to come in and have a chat with you?"

"Oh, I see." Mrs Abbott peered over her shoulder and called out, "Warren, come quickly. It's the police." She turned back and stood behind the door. "Come in. Have you found her? She never disappears like that. She's been missing since Saturday. We've been beside ourselves since we registered her missing."

Hero issued a half-smile. "Maybe we should go through to the lounge."

"Oh my. It's bad news, isn't it? Warren, damn you, get down here, now."

Her husband came thundering down the stairs. "Where's the damn fire? I was in the toilet, woman."

"I don't want to know, neither do they. Didn't you hear me? I told you the police were here." She turned her husband around and pushed him ahead of her. "Get in the lounge."

Hero had to restrain himself from chuckling at the way the man appeared to be henpecked. Fay would never treat him like that. He was grateful he had a wife who understood his needs and treated him respectfully.

The couple sat next to each other on the sofa. Julie and Hero each sat in an easy chair opposite the Abbotts. Hero's gaze drifted to the wall above the mantelpiece. On it was a painting of a young woman who he guessed to be Suzanna Abbott. She was stunning. She had long, flaming-red curly hair and glistening dark-green eyes, her skin as pale as that of most redheads he knew.

He glanced back at the couple, whose hands were tightly clenched around each other's. There was no easy way to break the news. He inhaled a large breath and let it seep out slowly. "It is with regret that I have to share with you some bad news. Earlier this morning, the body of a woman was found down at Salford Quays. We have reason to believe it's the body of your daughter, Suzanna Abbott."

Mrs Abbott screamed, and her husband placed an arm around her shoulder and hugged her tightly. "It'll be all right, love."

His wife pulled away and glared at him. "Will it? How is that possible? She's dead. No one can bring her back to us, Warren."

Mr Abbott faced Hero and demanded, "How do you know it's her? Don't you usually ask a relative to formally identify their next of kin?"

"Usually, yes." He sighed and gulped down the fluid filling his mouth. "We believe your daughter had a distinctive tattoo, is that correct?"

"Yes. Damn foolish girl, I told her not to get it done. She regretted it after a few days. Instead of getting rid of the bastard who dumped her and ran off with her money, she was lumbered with him for the rest of her... life."

Julie scrolled through her phone, located the picture of the tattoo and showed it to the father.

He nodded. "Yes, that's the one. Oh God. I can't believe she's no longer with us. How did she die? Was it an accident? I've told her so many bloody times to get a car that was more roadworthy than her old Mini, but she wouldn't listen to me."

"Hush, let the officer speak, Warren," his wife chastised him.

"I'm afraid we're conducting a murder inquiry into your daughter's death."

27

Mr Abbott jumped to his feet. "What? How? Who bloody did this? I'll kill the bastard."

"We've yet to figure that part out, sir. Our investigation only got underway a few hours ago."

"Jesus!" His wife pulled him back down beside her.

"Warren, can you just listen to what the officer has to say? I need to know what happened to my baby without you interrupting and kicking off every five seconds."

"Pardon me for breathing. Go on, you have my full attention now. How did she die?"

"It's not for me to really go into the details. Take my word for it, they're too gruesome to even contemplate hearing."

"What's that supposed to mean? Why are you refusing to tell us?" Mr Abbott shouted.

"I wouldn't want to hear the ins and outs of how my baby died," Mrs Abbott admitted. "Please don't tell us."

"I won't. I don't think it would be right for me to share the details with you anyway. What I will say is that the tattoo was the only thing we had to identify your daughter. There was no ID found at the crime scene."

"No bag, driving licence et cetera?" Warren asked.

"Nothing. Maybe you can tell us if your daughter has mentioned if she's had any problems recently?"

"You're talking about relationship problems, aren't you?" Mrs Abbott said.

"Yes. What about the man's name on the tattoo, can you tell us who he is and what happened there?"

"They split up over two years ago. The toerag was cheating on her with her best friend, Gina—she's no longer her friend now, or she wasn't. Gosh, I can't talk about her in the past tense, my brain won't allow me to do it, not yet," Mrs Abbott admitted. She wiped away the tears with a tissue and tucked it up her sleeve.

Hero nodded. "Can I ask if Suzanna had seen either of them lately?"

"No. I believe James moved to Liverpool, he left Gina behind in the end. It turned out to be a fling which damaged an excellent relationship. Gina and Suzanna had been childhood friends, grew up together, were always in and out of each other's houses. Shame on him, them, for treating our daughter that way, it was disgusting."

"What's his surname? I don't suppose you have a current address for him, do you?"

The Abbotts both shook their heads.

"No address. It's James Flitch. He works in a gym as a fitness trainer, if that helps," Warren told them.

"It does. Thank you. Has your daughter perhaps mentioned someone following her home from work recently? Sorry, I should have asked, where did she work?"

"She worked for a leasing company as a secretary. No, she didn't hint at anything being wrong. We were extremely close to our daughter. She had enough freedom to live her life as she wanted but knew she could count on us for support when she needed it. I can't believe she's gone and we'll never see her beautiful face again." Mrs Abbott looked at the painting on the wall. "That was commissioned when she was twenty-one as a surprise for her. She loved it but insisted it should remain here with us when she moved out. I loved her so much, she was so kind and considerate. A joy to be around, although lately, she's become far more wary of people after what James and Gina did to her."

"I can understand that. I don't suppose you know Gina's surname or have her address lying around anywhere?"

"I have. In my address book, I'll just get it. I never throw them out in case I need an address in the future." She rose from her chair and opened a small cabinet in the corner of the room. She returned to her seat and flicked through the pretty pink book. "Ah, here you are. Gina Crabtree. I should have remembered such an unusual name. I suppose I can be forgiven in the circumstances."

"You can. Please don't feel bad. Her address, do you have that as well?"

"Yes, it's eighteen Oxlade Road, Openshaw."

"That's fantastic. I can't thank you enough."

"You can thank us by finding whoever did this to our child," Mr Abbott said. He shook his head, clearly still stunned by the news Hero had delivered.

"We're going to do our very best," Hero promised.

"What's the next step for us now? When can we see her?" Mrs Abbott asked, hesitantly, as if she wanted to see her daughter but was afraid to, at the same time.

"I'll pass on your details to the pathologist. Gerrard will be in touch with you within the next few days. Then your daughter's body will be released and sent to the funeral directors."

"Can we start making the arrangements, or is it too soon?" Mr Abbott asked. "Only I hate the thought of us just sitting here doing nothing, waiting to get permission."

"I think it would be okay for you to make tentative enquiries, although, in my opinion, I would leave it a few days if I were you."

"Have you been in our situation, Inspector?" Warren demanded.

"Not exactly, no. But I've had to share this kind of tragic news more times than I care to remember, and every family deal with their grief differently. All I'm trying to say, is take things easy. There's no major panic as I don't think Suzanna's body will be released by the pathologist for some time. He'll need to carry out a lot of tests before that happens." *Jesus, what else can I bloody tell them other than keep it evasive?*

Mrs Abbott clenched her husband's hand. "We understand. Thank you for informing us. You'll be wanting to get out there to continue the investigation now, won't you?"

"Yes, but only if you and your husband are okay. Are you?"

"We'll have to be," Warren said, sharply. "I'm sorry, all this is so hard to take in. Our daughter was one of a kind. Thoughtful and generous to a fault. I just hope she wasn't killed because of her kindness and always doing the right thing by people."

"We hope that's not the case, too. Sorry, I forgot to ask, the leasing company she worked for, can you tell me where that is, please?"

"In the heart of the city. Leeman's Leasing is in Deansgate, if that helps?" Warren confirmed.

Hero rose from his seat, and Julie followed suit. "It does. We'll head off now, unless you need to ask us anything else?"

"Can't think of anything." Mr Abbott had already made his way to the door to see them out.

"Very well. We'll be in touch soon. Again, sorry for your loss, Mrs Abbott."

She looked up and offered a faint smile. "We're trusting you to find whoever took our child from us, Inspector."

"Don't worry. My team and I will be working around the clock to find them, I assure you."

"That's good to know." She wiped her eyes on another tissue, and they left her staring at the painting of her beloved daughter on the wall.

Mr Abbott had the front door open when they stepped into the hall. "Please, I'm asking you to go the extra mile for us. Whoever did this deserves to be punished. Our daughter wasn't the type to get into trouble. I didn't want to say this in front of my wife, but Suzanna has never done drugs or ended up so paralytic that she couldn't find her way home from the pub. She was a genuine person, responsible to a fault, if that helps. The person who has robbed us of our little girl needs to be dealt with as soon as possible."

"We're on the case, sir." Hero shook his hand and nodded. "We'll be in touch as soon as we've found a possible lead."

"Thank you, we'd appreciate that, Inspector. All we can ask is that you do your best for us."

"We will. I wouldn't still be in my role if I couldn't guarantee that."

"I suppose." He closed the door gently behind them.

Hero and Julie walked back to the car. Halfway there, Hero shook the tension out of his arms and rotated his head to ease the stiffness. "I really hate that part. Onwards and upwards, we have a few leads to follow up on."

Julie glanced down at her notebook once they were seated in the car. "Are you going to delegate some of them?"

"Yes, getting on to that now. I'll ask Jason to track down James. Get him to go see the man in Liverpool, if that's where he works now. It's not that far, better to get it out of the way early." He punched in a number which directed him straight to the incident room. "Yeah, it's me. Jason, I need you to get on the road again, sorry. Wait, what did you obtain from the CCTV, anything?"

"Only been back a few minutes, boss, but one of the shops had some interesting footage to share with us. I asked them to make a copy. It shows a white van pulling up in the early hours of this morning, throwing its rear doors open and disposing of the body."

"That's great news. Why do I hear a but in the air?"

"You can imagine, sir, no vehicle registration number, so they're keen on covering their tracks."

"Bugger, all right. What about the driver or the person in the back, did you get a good look at them? Tell me you did."

"Sorry to disappoint you. The one in the back was dressed all in black and wore a balaclava."

"They sound like utter professionals to me. Why cut her up and go to the bother of dumping her body in plain sight? It doesn't make sense."

"My thoughts exactly, sir. I was about to sift through the ANPR footage around the time the van was seen at the quay, but if you have other priorities for me, I can hand that particular task over to Foxy."

"Yes, do that. I need you to find out where a James Flitch works, he's a gym instructor in the Liverpool area. I know, big area to search, but you've got this. Once you've located him, I need you to go over there and question him in person."

"I can do that. Who is he, boss?"

"The former boyfriend of the victim. We're just on our way to see the victim's *former* best friend. Yes, you've guessed it, James and Gina had an affair, but they've since broken up. James has since moved to Liverpool. We'll find Gina and interview her. I need you to get an alibi from James, see what he was up to at the weekend. Maybe even ask if he has access to a white van."

"Leave it with me. I'll go now."

"Report back as soon as you've spoken to him. Good luck."

"Will do. Thanks, boss."

Hero ended the call and told Julie, "Satnav code for Gina first, I think, and then we'll drop by Suzanna's place of work. I hope it's easy to get to and we don't get caught up in traffic, you know what Deansgate can be like during the damned day."

Julie looked up the postcode on her phone and read it out for Hero to input into the satnav. Once that was done, they set off.

"What's running through your mind at this stage?" his partner asked.

Hero released a heavy sigh. "Not much in all honesty. The crime is far too vicious for 'normal people' to carry out, wouldn't you agree?"

"I was thinking along the same lines. We still need to speak to the ex-boyfriend and ex-friend, though, to discount them from the investigation. What if one of them has got into the wrong crowd and Suzanna was the one who ended up getting punished?"

"Possibly, although I think that's unlikely. Months have passed since they split up. It's a tough one. We could be guilty of wasting our time, but on the other hand, we won't know that until we've spoken to the individuals concerned."

"Bummer, isn't it? Why is it we never have a run-of-the-mill type of crime to deal with?"

He faced her briefly and smiled then turned back to the road ahead. "That's down to the criminals involved, they're definitely getting cannier these days. I can't get that image out of my head, of the victim. She was beautiful. Why go above and beyond in the gore stakes to brutalise another human being in such a horrendous way?"

"To prove a point?"

"Possibly. Either way, when we discover who's behind the crime, you're going to need to hold me back, because I'll want to wipe the floor with the bastard."

"I think you'll need to stand in line."

3

They reached Oxlade Road within ten minutes. Hero got out of the car and told Julie to remain behind, because he had a feeling it was going to be a waste of time and that Gina wasn't going to be home. His intuition proved to be correct. He rang the bell to the house next door. A young woman holding a toddler answered it.

Hero offered up his ID. "Sorry to disturb you. I'm looking for Gina who lives next door, any idea where she is?"

The woman frowned and jiggled the baby when he wriggled like a worm in her arms. "Why? What's she done?"

"Nothing as far as I know. It's a general enquiry. I don't suppose you know where she works, do you?"

"I do, as it happens."

The woman stopped talking.

Hero pinned his best smile in place. "Are you going to tell me?"

"What's it worth?"

"Excuse me?"

The woman's eyes narrowed. "Not that, you dirty bugger. I meant we've got problems with older kids in this area causing mischief. You promise to sort them out for me, and I'll tell you where she works."

"Oh right, sorry, crossed wires there for a moment. I can place a call to the station. Arrange for a couple of patrol cars to drive by now and again, if that will help?"

"It's better than nothing. She works at that posh shoe shop in the city."

Hero shrugged. "That could be anywhere, does this shop have a name?"

"Smart Shoes, I think it's called." The child started crying. "Sorry, gotta fly, this one needs changing."

"Good luck with that. Thanks for your help."

Before she closed the door, she pointed out at the road. "Don't go back on your promise now, will you?"

"I'll get on the blower now."

"Good, it's about time you lot made yourselves useful." With that, she slammed the door in his face.

"Charming. It was a pleasure making your acquaintance, too," he mumbled on the way back to the car.

Julie was scrolling through her phone when he slipped into the vehicle. "At it again, I see."

"It's to do with work. I'm searching for the postcode for the leasing company, if you must know."

"Sorry. I should have asked first, instead of jumping to conclusions. Gina wasn't at home, and her super-helpful neighbour told me she works at that posh shoe shop in town."

"Which one? Smart Shoes?"

"Get you. How did you know that?"

"I've been known to set foot in the shop now and again. Mum used to get most of her shoes from there when she was alive."

"Sorry, I didn't mean to sound so off-hand. I suppose you still miss her."

"Hard not to. She was my life. When I wasn't working, I used to be there, doing everything for her. I go home now at the end of my shift and I feel guilty if I have an evening of just putting my feet up. I know how much you hate Rob, but he treats me right. We're partners around the house, he doesn't take advantage of me, not in that respect," she added, blushing.

"I'm glad to hear it. You deserve to be treated like a princess after caring for your mother all those years, Julie."

Julie looked at him, dazed. "Did those words just come out of your mouth?"

Hero chuckled. "I'm not a grouch all the time, you should know that by now. Here we go then."

He left the parking space and headed into the sprawling metropolis he had mixed feelings about. Most days he loved living in Manchester, if he could manage to steer clear of the city centre, where they were heading.

The shop they were after was located in a small line of exclusive shops. There was a car park opposite, so Hero dumped his car there and, together, he and Julie crossed the road. The shop had two customers browsing and two shop attendants on hand to satisfy their needs.

Hero approached the older woman manning the till at the rear. "Hello there. DI Nelson and DS Shaw. Would it be possible to speak with Gina, please?"

The woman swiftly turned in the younger woman's direction. "Gina, these people are here to see you." She lowered her voice to add, "They're the police."

Gina frowned and stepped forward. "The police? Have I done something wrong?"

"Is there somewhere we can chat in private?"

"Yes, go. Use my office if you have to," the older woman suggested.

Gina motioned for Hero and Julie to join her. "Thanks, Sylvie. Hopefully I won't be too long. If you'd like to come this way."

Hero smiled at Sylvie. "We won't keep her longer than is necessary, I promise."

"Good. There needs to be two of us here at all times, to act as a deterrent, you know."

"I do. Quite right, too." He followed Gina and Julie through a small stockroom to an equally less-than-generous office that only contained one chair.

Gina sat behind the desk and asked, "What's going on? What's this about?"

"We're making general enquiries into a crime that was committed this morning," Hero began. He watched Gina's reaction carefully. All was good so far, she just seemed perplexed about them being there.

"Go on. What sort of crime? I hope you're not suggesting I had anything to do with it."

"That's what we intend to find out. Maybe you can tell us where you were over the weekend?"

"What? No, not until you tell me what it is I'm supposed to have done."

Hero cocked an eyebrow at her. "It's a simple question. Please answer it as fully as you can."

"I was helping a friend of mine move house. I stayed over for a few days with her to get the place straight. I haven't been back home since Friday morning. Now, I repeat, what's this about, and why are you harassing me like this?"

"I wouldn't necessarily say we're harassing you, Gina. Do you have a contact number for your friend so we can verify your alibi?"

"Jesus, really? It's in my phone which is locked in the canteen. Want me to get it?"

"If you wouldn't mind. Come straight back, please do not contact your friend in the meantime."

"What the…?" Gina stormed out of the room and returned within a few moments, her mobile in her hand. She scrolled through her contacts and handed the phone to Julie. "Here, Fiona is her name. That's her number."

"Julie, would you mind ringing Fiona to verify the facts?"

"Of course." Julie left the room to make the call.

"This is ridiculous. I demand to know why you're treating me this way."

"All we've done so far is ask you to verify your whereabouts. I apologise if you've taken that as an intrusion. It's important."

"Why? What's important enough to warrant you coming to my place of work?"

"Take a seat, Gina."

The young woman growled and threw herself into the chair. Julie re-entered the room and nodded. "It's the truth."

"Of course it bloody well is. Now, tell me why you're here or I'm going to report you for coming here and hounding me. I'm innocent. I've never done anything against the law, except…"

Hero's interest piqued; he inclined his head. "Except?"

"That time I was caught for shoplifting when I was nine. It was a mistake. Is that what this is about? You've finally caught up with me after all these years?"

Hero smiled, doing his best to put Gina at ease. "If you'd just calm down for a moment, we'll explain. And no, this has nothing to do with your shoplifting experience." He wagged a finger at her. "Please don't do that again."

"I won't. I've learnt my lesson. So why are you here?"

"When was the last time you saw Suzanna Abbott?"

Gina fell back in her chair. "Golly, it must be a few months. Around March, she blanked me in the street for what happened. And yes, I regret how things went down. It was an isolated incident, and we all paid the price."

"You sleeping with James, is that what you're getting at?"

"That's right. I was drunk at the time. He came on to me, and we ended up in bed together. Neither of us continued the relationship. Like I said, it was a one-off, a drunken mistake that cost me the best friend I've ever had."

"Did you try to patch things up with her?"

"I did. She was having none of it. We've both moved on, and I believe, the last time I heard, James even relocated to Liverpool. Good riddance to him. I've regretted that mistake ever since. But what has this got to do with why you're here?"

He inhaled then let the breath seep out. "We're here because we're conducting a murder inquiry."

"What? Who's been bloody murdered? Oh God, not James?"

"No. Sorry to have to tell you this, but Suza—"

"No!" Gina bounced forward in her chair and screamed. "She can't be dead. I don't believe you."

The door suddenly flew open, and the older woman appeared. "What the hell is going on in here? Gina?"

"I'm sorry. I didn't mean to scream. I've had some shocking news."

"Oh, I see. Well, perhaps you'll keep the noise down in future. Think about the customers." She huffed out a breath and slammed the door as she left.

Gina stared past Hero at the door. "Insensitive bitch. I hate her at times."

"Not the best response I've ever heard from an employer, I grant you," Hero admitted. "Are you okay?"

"Would you be, hearing that shitty news? I'm sorry, I don't mean to take this out on you. I'm in shock, it's dreadful news. I hope you've found the person responsible?"

"Not yet. Our investigation is still in its infancy. What can you tell me about Suzanna?"

"In what way? She was my friend for years." She lowered her head and picked up a paperclip which she ran through her fingers as she spoke. "Until I did the dirty on her. Fuck, I feel even worse about my traitorship now that she's de... I can't say the word. Now that she's gone. Murder, you say? Can I ask how she died? Do I even want to know?"

"No, for a start, we can't reveal the facts, not yet, and for another, the truth is too gruesome to share with you or anyone else. When was the last time you saw Suzanna, to speak to, I mean?"

"Oh heck! I remember the day well. It was when she found us in bed, you know, me in bed with James. She shouted at us both, told us she never wanted to see either of us again. I tried to ring her several times, but she refused to accept my calls. I even called around to her house, but again, she looked out of the window, saw me standing on the doorstep, stuck two fingers up at me and drew the curtains. I got the hint after that and haven't tried to contact her in any way, shape or form since." She shook her head and fiddled with the paperclip, weaving it frantically through her fingers. "What have I done? Is she dead because of me?"

Hero glanced sideways and sensed Julie looking his way. He turned his attention back to Gina and asked, "What do you mean by that?"

Her head rose, and Gina's gaze met his. "No, is that why you're here? You think I had something to do with her death? No, I could never do that. Please... you have to believe me. Oh God, please don't arrest me. I've done nothing wrong. I swear I haven't. Well, except sleep with her fella. Not that I can even remember that either. I was drunk at the time."

Hero raised his hands to prevent her from stressing more than she was already. "Calm down. We're not here to arrest you, however, we do want you to help us with our enquiries, if you're willing?"

"Of course. But how? Name it and I'll do it for you, for Suzanna. I'll do anything if it'll help you find her killer."

"Good, thank you. When you were friends, say towards the end of your friendship, did she mention that she was in any kind of trouble?"

Gina's features wrinkled as she thought. "I don't think so. We were really close, she would have told me if anything was bugging her."

"What about James?"

Gina shuddered at the mention of his name. "What about him? No, you don't think he's capable of doing this? He couldn't be. He wouldn't!"

"We're going to have a chat with him. Maybe, maybe not, we won't know that until we speak with him. Do you think he would have hated Suzanna enough to have wanted to end her life?"

"No, not in a million years. He always came across as more of a lover than a fighter kind of guy to me, if you get my drift. But then again, he moved to Liverpool, what's to stop him coming back to Manchester to do the deed and then going back to Liverpool?"

"Indeed. But you reckon it's not in his character to do such a thing, right?"

"Yeah, that's right. Hey, I wouldn't want to get him into trouble or anything. Not because I fancy him, I just don't think he has it in him to take someone's life. But hey, what do I really know about what goes on in someone's head?"

"Exactly. Hence us needing to have a chat with him. Perhaps you can give us a little insight into what sort of character Suzanna was?"

"She was fun to be with. Wouldn't harm a soul. Never really spoke badly of anyone, not until they wronged her, like I did. I got what I deserved and a lot more besides. If she'd done the dirty on me, though, I would have forgiven her. I know that's easy to say, but I would have. She meant a lot to me. Which makes me feel even worse in the long run. I should have kept my legs shut and rejected James' advances towards me. Bloody hell, I can't believe she's gone. Why? That's what I can't figure out. Why would some fucker pick her? Do you think she started dating someone else, you know, after James? Could that person be guilty of killing her?"

"It's definitely on our list to try and find out. Can you tell us if she was close to anyone else? Another friend she would have confided in, if she no longer had you in her life?"

"I don't think so. We were more like sisters. I know that makes matters seem worse still and, believe me, the whole debacle has kept me awake at night, mulling things over, I can assure you."

"I can imagine. What about at work? Was she close to anyone there perhaps?"

"I think she mentioned a woman called Kath, who was more like a mother figure to her. Slightly older, she is. She might be able to fill in the gaps for you. I'm sorry I can't. As much as I want to help you, I've told you everything I know now."

"That's okay. We're sorry to have broken the news to you in such a way that you found it upsetting." Hero cringed at the words he used.

Gina nodded. "You did what you had to do. I only wish I could help you with your investigation. I've lost a good friend. I'm sure we would have overcome our differences eventually. She really wasn't the type to hold a grudge for long. I'll miss her."

"Thanks for your help. I'll leave you a card, should you think of anything else you feel is relevant to our enquiries." He slid a business card across the desk.

"Thank you. I'd better get back to work now."

"You're free to do that. Thanks for sparing us the time."

Gina shoved back her chair and passed Hero to open the door. "I hope you find them... whoever did this to her. She didn't deserve to go out this way."

"No one does, I can assure you."

Julie followed Hero out of the shop, trotting to keep up with his determined long strides. "What did you make of her?" his partner asked.

"She appeared genuine enough to me. Why? Something off to you?"

"I often have suspicions about people if they're willing to do the dirty on their best friend, like she did."

"Hmm... fair enough point. Let's keep her on the list for now, in case nothing else shows up."

"On to the leasing firm now?"

"Might as well as we're out and about. It's only around the corner, I believe. Are you up for a walk?"

"Only if you refrain from steaming ahead of me."

Hero looked at Julie's lower half. "Sorry, I should have remembered you've only got short legs. Trouble is, when a case is rattling around in my mind, I forget myself and the fact you're with me, apparently."

"Don't think I hadn't noticed," Julie grumbled.

They walked, more sedately this time, past the local shops.

Julie hesitated outside a fancy baker's on the high street. "These look divine."

"Probably cost a packet as well. If you're good I'll treat you to a cream slice on the way back."

"Wow, I'll hold you to that."

A few feet later, they had reached the offices of the leasing company. Hero pushed the front door and held it open for his partner to enter. There were five desks in the glass-fronted area. A woman in her forties, wearing small-rimmed glasses approached them.

"Hello, how can I help?"

Hero and Julie produced their IDs. "DI Nelson and DS Shaw. Is the manager or owner of the business around?"

"I'm the office manager for the branch. We're a national company with branches in fifty-odd towns. What do you need to know?"

"Sorry, I didn't catch your name."

"It's Kath Beddows."

"Ah, in that case, I think you're the lady we're after."

"Really? Have I done something wrong?"

"No. Is there somewhere private we can chat?"

"Of course. There's a restroom out the back. Come through."

She turned, and they followed her under the gaze of the other four members of staff, seated at their desks.

"Take a seat." She collected two more chairs from the pile in the corner and set them out in front of her. She then sat in the only other vacant chair in the room. "What's this about?"

"I'm afraid we have some bad news for you."

Kath frowned and covered her mouth with her hand, easing it down eventually to ask, "Is it about my husband? Has he had an accident? I told him the car didn't sound right when we went out on Saturday."

"No, it's nothing like that. It's about a work colleague of yours. Suzanna Abbott."

"Oh my. She was due in this morning. I've tried to call her several times, I thought it was strange she didn't pick up. Please, tell me, is she in hospital?"

Hero sighed. "Yes, unfortunately, she's in the mortuary. Suzanna died over the weekend."

Kath's eyes bulged, and her hand shook as she touched her face. "Oh no. I can't believe I'm hearing this. How?" Tears slipped from her bright-blue eyes onto her colourless cheeks.

"I'm sorry this has hit you so hard. I'm afraid Suzanna was murdered."

"Are you sure? Murdered? Doesn't that sort of thing only happen in Hollywood?"

"No, you'd be surprised. Can I get you a glass of water?"

"Yes, please. My cup has my name on it, it's in the cupboard above the sink."

Hero fetched the water and returned to his seat. She took the water from him and downed half of it in one gulp.

Wiping her mouth, Kath asked, "Did she suffer? Before her death, I mean."

"It's not possible for us to know that for sure. Let's go along the lines that she didn't, it might be better for you to deal with the news."

"Yes, let's do that. Where was she found?"

"Down by Salford Quays. Were you two very close?"

"Close enough. She didn't deserve to die, especially after what she's been through."

"May I ask what you're referring to?"

"That ghastly best friend and former boyfriend of hers. They did the dirty behind her back, and she lost both of them. I know it was a while ago, but she was devastated by their betrayal. I was the one who sat with her, consoling her for weeks on end. She used to be in tears during her coffee break most days. I tried to tell her they weren't worth it and to move on. I think my words finally sank in. To my astonishment, she signed up to one of those online dating sites. I tried to dissuade her, but one of the blokes working here assured her it was quite safe and that's how he'd met his girlfriend. It was news to us at the time."

Hero nodded slowly as her words sank in. "I see. That's interesting. Do you know which site?"

"Rod will be able to tell you that."

"We'll ask on the way out. Do you know if she'd had any success on the site?"

"Yes, a few men were interested in taking her out. She'd started speaking to a couple of possible candidates…" She clicked her fingers. "Actually, she was due to meet up with one of them on Saturday night. Shit! Sorry for swearing, not like me at all to do that. Do you think the person she met murdered her?"

"Possibly, it's looking likely. You're saying she'd held conversations with a couple of men. I'm not sure how these sites work; would the other men have been able to have seen the conversations she was holding?"

"Oh no, I don't believe so. I think that sort of thing takes place through private messages. I'm far too old to grasp the ins and outs of online dating. Should I ask Rod to speak to you? He'll be better informed than me on the topic."

"Okay, if it'll make you feel more comfortable."

She stood and left the room, returning accompanied by the ginger young man they had passed on their way in. "This is Rod. I haven't told him anything."

Hero jumped out of his chair and positioned himself by the sink. "Take a seat, Rod, we'd like to ask you a few questions regarding your experience on the dating site you used."

"Okay. That's a strange request. Has something happened that I should know about?"

"We'll get to that soon. Maybe you can run through how the site works?"

"It's all above board, I promise. I met Lucy on it around six months ago. We're blissfully happy, so much so that I'm about to pop the question. We've been living with each other for the past two months, and we're going from strength to strength." He smiled at the prospect.

"Excellent news. So how did you meet Lucy? Run me through the procedure, if you will?"

"You register, put in your bio, make it snappy—no one wants to know if you're boring on your profile, that'll make you seem unattractive. You list your hobbies and places you like to go, and that's it really. You sit back and wait for all the attention to come your way, or not! I was lucky, Lucy and I got together after I'd been registered for only a week or so. I couldn't believe my luck."

"How do you know people are real and not just hiding behind a fake persona?" Hero asked, folding his arms.

"I think it's far less of a risk these days, there are stringent security questions. Saying that, I wasn't trying to be evasive or set out to trick anyone, so someone with bad intentions might know how to falsify things and get away with it. Maybe these sites are open to being

45

manipulated, which put me off joining an online dating site for a few years, if I'm honest."

"What changed your mind?"

"A friend of mine met his girlfriend through the site, which persuaded me to take the plunge."

"Okay, and then you passed on the site details to Suzanna Abbott, is that correct?"

Rod's brow crumpled. "Yes. Has something happened to Suzanna? I noticed she wasn't at work today but never thought anything more about it."

"She's dead," Kath whispered.

"No!" Rod raked a hand through his short hair. "I don't believe it. Shit! Does this have anything to do with the site? I'd never be able to forgive myself if it turned out she'd met someone on there."

"We're not sure. All we know at this stage is that she was murdered. How and who did it are what we're trying to figure out. Did she mention who she was meeting on Saturday?"

"No names were mentioned. She told me the guy sounded too good to be true and that she was looking forward to meeting him. Damn, she was a lovely lady, full of… life. I can't believe she's gone. So sorry, Kath, I know you and Suzanna were close friends."

"Thanks, we were. Although she still kept me at arm's length occasionally. I didn't take offence to that, not after what she went through with her best friend. It was understandable she wouldn't want to get too close."

"Okay, thank you both, you've been really helpful. Rod, can you give me the details of the site?"

"Of course."

Julie handed the young man her notebook, and he jotted down the name and gave it back to her.

"Is there anything else either of you can tell us? Such as whether Suzanna mentioned being worried about something. Someone following her, perhaps?"

Rod and Kath glanced at each other and shook their heads. "No, nothing like that, not as far as I can remember. Maybe something will ring a bell later, after you've gone and my head is a bit straighter than it is right now." Kath rubbed at her temple with her thumb and forefinger.

"I'll give you one of my cards, just in case. Rod?"

"No, sorry. I wasn't that close to her. I doubt if she would have confided in me anyway."

"Okay. We'll leave it there, then. If anything should come to mind, no matter how insignificant you believe it to be, will you call me?" He gave them both a card.

"Of course we will. What about the other staff? Would you like to speak to them as well? Might be worth it," Kath suggested.

"Yes, why not? It can't do any harm. Thank you both for talking with us. Can you send the staff in one by one?"

"I'll do that," Kath replied as they both left.

"Damned online dating sites, worst invention ever," Hero mumbled.

"They have their uses, sometimes. Look at Rod, he found love through the site."

"Yeah, but what if it turns out that Suzanna met her killer through the damned site? What then? How the hell are we going to track down all those who were interested in her? If she registered in her own name, it wouldn't take much for a calculating individual to find out her home address, would it? He wouldn't need to make contact with her on the site, would he?"

"That is devious but accurate, I suppose. We'll know more when we start digging."

"Can you bring it up on that damned phone of yours?"

Julie entered the name of the site into the search engine and angled the phone his way. "Seems professional enough."

A knock on the door interrupted them.

"Come in," Hero shouted.

A blonde woman in her thirties appeared in the doorway. "Kath asked me to drop by and see you. How can I help? I'm Emma by the way."

"Hello, Emma, did Kath tell you why?" Hero motioned for the young woman to take a seat.

"Sadly, she told us that Suzanna is dead. We're all gutted to hear the news. Not sure what I can do to help, but I'm willing to give it a go."

"Thank you for coming to see us. Did Suzanna mention something was troubling her at all?"

"When? Recently?"

"Yes, perhaps in the last few weeks or so?"

"No, not really. I knew she was upset after falling out with her best friend. I'm not sure what that was about, I wouldn't say we were that close, not really. We don't have time to sit around and gossip. Kath always keeps us on the go during the day. She's a tough taskmaster."

"I see. As far as we know, her best friend was caught in bed with her boyfriend."

"Blimey! How cruddy is that? Poor Suzanna, no wonder she didn't really trust people."

"Did she tell you that?"

"No, I just got the impression something major had happened. I suppose she became withdrawn a little for a few months. But something changed a couple of weeks ago. She seemed a lot brighter for some reason. I overheard her and Rod discussing the online dating scene and presumed she'd possibly joined the same site where he met Lucy."

"I see. Thanks for the confirmation. Okay, you can go. Can you send the next person in?"

"I will. Sorry I couldn't help any further."

"It's fine."

She left, and Hero stared out of the window at the back yard. "Everything seems to be pointing to the site at this stage, agreed?"

"Yeah. No one's told us the name of the fella she was due to meet yet, have they?"

Hero narrowed his eyes as he thought and turned to face Julie. "That's right. As soon as we leave here, we need to get on to the site, see if they're willing to tell us. I know there are privacy laws on their side, but they go out of the window when we're investigating a murder case. Wait, no, leave the other two interviews to me, you go outside and place the call to the site. You know what to ask, right?"

Julie slammed her notebook shut and stood. "Of course I do, I'm not a novice." She stormed out of the room.

Hero cringed. *I never said you were. Me and my big mouth!*

Julie hadn't been gone long when the next member of staff joined him. Tracy sat in the chair opposite and looked shell-shocked by the news.

"Are you all right?" he asked.

"Would you be if you'd just been told someone you have worked alongside for three years had been murdered?"

"Okay, I understand where you're coming from. How well did you know Suzanna?"

"Not very well, apparently, from what I can gather, listening to the others."

"Meaning what?"

"I didn't know she had a date with someone she met online on Saturday, for starters."

"And if you'd known?"

"I would have tried to prevent her from going. I don't believe in those kinds of sites. They must be full of bad people, or is that me going over the top there?"

"I can't say I've had a lot of dealings with these types of sites in the past, either professionally or personally."

"Well, I have. Not me personally, but my cousin had a terrible time when she joined. One of the blokes wouldn't stop badgering her online. She told him to get lost; the next thing she knew, he was knocking on her front door, demanding to see her. Luckily, she'd met someone else, a copper actually. He was at the house when this guy called. He threatened to arrest him if he came anywhere near her again."

"And did he?" Hero scratched the stubble on his chin.

"No."

"Can you remember the bloke's name? Was it the same site?"

"Yes, I think it was. I could ring her, if that would help?"

"It would. Can you do it now?"

"I'll just get my phone, it's in my locker. Too much of a distraction to have it on my desk, Kath says."

Hero smiled and nodded. She darted across to the other side of the room to the tall bank of lockers and extracted her phone to place the call. "Hi, Mia, it's me. Just a quickie. You know that bother you had with that prick…" She grinned at Hero and mouthed an apology. "The one who came to your house… can you remember his name…? Sorry, I can't explain now… I'll ring you at lunchtime. Thanks. Speak later. Yes, everything is fine." She ended the call and returned the phone to her locker. "It was Kevin Dunster. She got all flustered when I brought the incident up. It truly affected her badly at the time."

"Sorry to hear that. Is she still with the copper?"

"Oh yes. They make a lovely couple. Do you need anything else from me?"

"No, thanks very much for the information. Can you send the final lady in?"

She smiled and scampered out of the room. The last member of staff was in tears when she arrived. So much so that Hero couldn't work out what she was saying half the time. Therefore, he cut the interview short and sent her packing. He left the room, had a quick chat with Kath on the way out, and then joined Julie outside. She was grinning when he approached her.

"Good news, I take it?"

"Yes, their offices are just around the corner. I'm on the phone to Priscilla Jordan now, she runs the site."

"Tell her we'll call round and see her in person."

"Already in hand. Just getting the address now."

4

---

*P*riscilla Jordan lived up to her name. She was dressed smartly in a haute couture suit that screamed it cost around five grand to purchase.

"Oh, I wasn't expecting you to turn up so soon. When you said you were around the corner, I thought you were having me on," the woman said, her voice as posh as her suit.

"Is there a problem?" Hero inclined his head but didn't smile. The woman appeared slightly jumpy to him; he intended to keep her on her toes throughout this interview.

"Not at all. Come through to my office."

She led them into a swish office. It had floor-to-ceiling glass on three sides. On the desk was an open Apple MacBook. Priscilla took her seat behind the desk. Hero noted she didn't shut the computer down but glanced at it now and again. Over time, he knew this would tick him off.

"Any chance you can close your computer while we speak? I can already see it's going to be a form of distraction for you."

"No, I'm sorry. I have a compulsive disorder where my business is concerned. I freak out if I don't keep an eye on it twenty-four hours a day."

Hero frowned. "Are you telling me you don't sleep?"

"I suppose I am. Well, very rarely. I'm addicted to the site, the workings of it, and I love to see the number of people joining notch up hourly."

"I see. Have you ever thought about getting help for your obsession?"

"Oh no. I don't really class it as such, not really. I'm proud, you see. For years people have been crying out for a site like mine, therefore I'm extremely proud of the service I provide."

"I don't understand. Enlighten us as to why your site is different from any other dating site on this planet."

"I have exceptional security. I pride myself on finding the perfect match for people, no half measures, they have to be perfect."

"And if they're not?"

"Then they don't get matched."

Hero scratched the side of his face. "How is that possible?"

"I ensured it. I paid for the best IT chappie to set up the system. He's actually a good friend of mine. We don't have riff-raff joining."

"Why? Because you charge an exorbitant fee?"

She laughed. "If you think a thousand pounds is high, you should visit some of the more exclusive sites that are around."

"They're higher than a grand to join?" Hero asked, shocked.

"Indeed, anything from five thousand to twenty-five thousand for a lifetime membership."

"Bloody hell, I had no idea it could cost that much to find love. What happened to walking into a pub and meeting someone down at the local?"

Priscilla laughed. It was a dainty laugh that grated on Hero for some reason. Julie sniggered beside him.

"I'm afraid those days are long gone, for those who are serious about settling down, I should say. People are searching for their soul mate, someone they're destined to be with for the rest of their lives. That's hardly likely to happen down at the nearest boozer now, is it?"

Hero shrugged. "I don't see why not. It's where I met my wife, and we've been together around twelve years now, I think."

"You think? That's a typical reaction from your gender. However, if you had joined my site and met the love of your life you would be one hundred percent sure of the significant dates in your life. Such as when you first met, when you got engaged, what date you got married."

"All right, I get your drift. Let's discuss the workings of your site in depth, shall we?"

She sat back, her gaze flitting over the screen briefly before her attention settled on Hero again. "What do you want to know?"

"Basically, how you can tell when a subscriber… is that what you call them?" She nodded and waved her hand. "How do you tell they're not fake accounts being created to entice people to fall for their lies?"

"Easy. With stringent security checks." Priscilla steepled her fingers.

"Stringent checks, such as what?"

"Financial, of course. We dig deep into their finances, it's all above board. They have to prove they are financially stable with a regular income coming in."

"And people divulge that kind of information freely?"

"Yes. All right, a few years ago when I first set up the site, the rules were very different back then, but I wanted this club to be elite, so felt I needed to change the way people signed up. If people don't like the way we work they have the option to walk away."

"But you still have members who were with you from the beginning when the signing up process was, more mundane, shall we say?"

"Yes, although there aren't that many who are active these days. In truth, I'm in the process of closing their accounts down."

"Why? When they've already paid upfront?"

"Because of the webspace involved in running the site, we're nearly at full capacity. If I don't cull the inactive members then it's going to cost me nearly a million to increase the capacity."

Hero whistled. "A million? Wow, I hope it's worth all the hassle?"

Priscilla studied the diamonds that were sitting proud on her fingers. "I think so, yes, although I'm doing my very best to cut costs down, obviously."

"I see. Which is why you keep a careful eye on your business, I get it now."

"This is definitely not a nine-to-five job. Most members are online from seven in the evening to around one or two in the morning. Hence the bags under my eyes."

"Don't you have staff who can monitor things for you?"

"I'm a control freak. I couldn't allow anyone to take over the reins, not even for a few hours."

"Okay. I get that, I think."

"Good. Why are you here?"

"We're conducting a murder inquiry and have reason to believe the deceased was a member of your site and had arranged to meet someone on a date on Saturday. Would it be possible for you to confirm that for us?"

"Gracious me. A murder victim? I can assure you I have no murderers trawling through my site."

"With due respect, Mrs Jordan, how do you know?"

The woman was stunned into silence for a second or two. She recovered and forced her shoulders back. "Because of what I've already told you, we carry out stringent searches on our members, clients, whatever you want to call them."

"Will you be able to tell us who the victim was in touch with?"

"I'm sorry. Not without a warrant to hand."

"Then I'll get one. Can you at least tell me if the victim was a member?"

She sat forward, fingers poised over the keyboard. "Name?"

"Suzanna Abbott."

She tapped a few keys and inclined her head as she peered at the screen. "Pretty lady. Yes, she was a member. Are you sure she was due to meet up with another of my clients and that she didn't belong to another site?"

"We're sure. We've just visited her work colleagues. Your site was suggested to her, and she signed up in the hope of finding her soul mate, one would assume. Are you sure you can't tell us who she had arranged a date with?"

Priscilla inhaled, her small chest inflating a little. "Go on then, I'm feeling in a generous mood."

Hero sighed internally. *Maybe I should try being off-hand more often, if this is the result.*

"Ah, here we go. Her profile says that she was in contact with a few men." She reached for a notebook and jotted something down then slid it across the desk towards Hero. "Three names for you to consider."

Hero's eyes widened. "Three, eh? Popular young lady."

"Not really. Some of our members are in touch with ten-plus members of the opposite sex."

"Big business this dating lark then?"

Priscilla smiled. "Very."

"Would it be cheeky of me to ask if you have the members' addresses on the system?"

"Yes, it would. I can't possibly give out that information and retain my good reputation, I'm sorry."

Hero waved away the apology. "Not a problem. We'll figure it out for ourselves. I'm so grateful for what you've given us."

"The only thing I ask is that you don't tell the men where you acquired their names from, is that possible?"

"Discretion is my middle name, well, that and Horatio." The woman sniggered. "I'm joking, of course." He rose from his chair and extended his hand for Priscilla to shake.

Outside, Hero and Julie began the walk back to the car. "I didn't think she was going to give up that information. Let's hope it proves to be the key we need to unlock this investigation."

"I was surprised as well. I think she fancied you."

Hero winced. "Are you winding me up, Shaw?"

"No, why would you think that? You're a good-looking fella, in the right light," she added with a chuckle.

"Thanks for the compliment, I think."

"My pleasure. Want me to get in touch with the station, see if they can trace the names for us?"

"Yes, get Foxy on it, she's got a talent for those kinds of searches."

Julie made the call as they continued their journey back to the car.

*A*fter picking up half a dozen cream cakes from the baker's, they arrived back at the station, Foxy had sourced the addresses of the three men. Julie handed the cakes around while Hero approached the whiteboard and brought the information up to date. He added the names, Martin Jessop, Gyles Gordon and Julian Hylton, to the right-hand side of the board as possible suspects. "What else have we got?"

"The van, which is at present without a registration number. The fact that two men were in the van, one driving and another dumping the body out of the back. Who's to say how many others were inside, though?" Julie added.

"Yes, all good stuff. Damn, I forgot to ask Priscilla about Kevin Dunster, the guy who stalked that woman's cousin at the leasing firm," Hero replied.

"Want me to see if he has a record?" Julie suggested.

"Yes, do that. See what comes back, and I'll run it past Priscilla, ask her if he's still on the site and whether he made any contact with Suzanna. I'm feeling positive about this, guys. Keep up the good work." He completed bringing the board up to date and then went back into his office. It was three o'clock in the afternoon, and he was beginning to flag after his early morning start to the day. He decided to ring home, needing to speak to Fay.

"Hey, how are you?"

"I'm fine. Just looking in the fridge to see what I can rustle up for dinner, any suggestions?"

"Sorry, not my department. Ouch, I didn't mean that, you know I'd help out if I had the time, love."

"I know that. What do you fancy?"

"Umm... sausage and chips will do me. You don't have to spend hours and hours cooking every day."

"I do it because I want the kids to have nutritional meals inside them. Okay, just this once. I don't want the kids to get used to eating such crap."

"I agree. I should be home at around six, maybe before if I can wangle it."

"Good, you shouldn't be expected to work to your normal hours if you commence nearly four hours before your shift was due to start. Sorry, you don't need to hear a lecture."

"You're right. Unfortunately, the powers that be don't see it that way."

"Never mind. I'm going to get on. I have to leave soon to pick up the twins."

"Oops... sorry, I forgot it was school kicking out time."

"You'd be no good as a stay-at-home dad, would you?"

He laughed. "So true. They'd look like a tin of baked beans before long if the dinners were left up to me. See you later. I love you, Fay Nelson."

"I know you do, I love you, too. Now go, leave me in peace."

"I know when I'm not wanted. See you later."

He ended the call and attended to another batch of post that had appeared on his desk whilst he was out. The rest of the afternoon consisted of chasing up the team for information. Time passed by quickly, even if the details proved to be thin on the ground.

Finally, he told the team to go home at just after six. On his journey back to the house, he twisted his neck from side to side to release the tension that had arisen during his hectic day. By the time he reached the house, all that tension had dispersed and he felt chilled enough to do the one thing he loved the most, play with the kids after a long, hard shift.

"Hi, everyone, I'm home," he announced, entering the front door.

Sammy was the first to greet him. He bounced up and down and tried to bark but he was getting old now and it was showing in his joints and his throat.

Hero bent down to stroke his beloved dog. "Hey, mate, did you miss me? I'll take you out for a walk in a while, I promise." Sammy rubbed against him, almost pushing Hero over in the process. "Cheeky sod. Stop shoving me, you mongrel."

"Daddy, Daddy, come play with us."

Zara and Zoe raced into the hall. Each of them grabbed an arm and, yanking him to his feet, they dragged him into the lounge. Set out on the floor was a vast array of Lego.

"Where did this lot come from?"

"Mum got it for us," Zoe replied. She flopped down on the floor, crossed her legs, picked up a couple of pieces and examined them closely.

"Did she now. I'll have to have a word with Mummy about that."

Fay cleared her throat in the doorway to the kitchen. He drifted towards her and kissed her on the lips. "What's that? The Lego? A friend gave it to me at the school gates. Don't worry, I disinfected it before I gave it to the girls to play with."

"Expensive stuff. Looks in good nick, though. Why did they want to get rid of it?" He tilted his head and noticed the usual sparkle was missing from her eyes. "Everything okay? You weren't expecting me to tell you off about spending money, were you?"

Fay placed a hand on his chest. "No. I know it's not in you to do that. I'll tell you later when small ears aren't around."

"Sounds ominous."

"Leave it for now, hon."

"Okay. If you insist. Where's Louie?"

She pointed to the ceiling. "In his room." Tears bulged in her beautiful eyes.

Hero placed a hand on her cheek and whispered, "You're worrying me now, love. What's wrong?"

"Nothing. Go and get changed, dinner won't be long."

"I've promised Sammy a walk. Maybe we can ask Louie to mind the girls for us after dinner and take a stroll down to the park."

"Maybe we could all go for a walk, I think the girls might enjoy that. Not sure about Louie, though."

"I'll check in on him and ask." He kissed her again and left the lounge. At the top of the stairs, he heard the sound of the bathroom lock engaging. He'd catch up with Louie after changing out of his suit. He pulled on a pair of sweatpants and a T-shirt and hung around for five minutes, anticipating his son's reappearance. Tired of waiting, he took the plunge and knocked on the bathroom door. "Son, is everything all right?"

Louie sniffled and said, "Yes, leave me alone."

"Are you okay? You don't sound all right to me. Open the door, let me in, son."

"No. I'm going to the toilet. Can't I do that in peace nowadays?"

"Of course you can. You sound upset to me. Come on, a problem shared and all that."

"I'm fine. I just want to be left alone."

"Okay. Dinner will be soon, we'll have a chat then, how about that?"

"Whatever." Another sniffle, and then Louie blew his nose.

Hero's heart shattered into a million pieces. He was desperate to help Louie, but his son obviously had other ideas. Instead, he gave up trying and went back downstairs where the girls were building a fairy-tale princess castle.

"Daddy, what's this part belong to?"

Hero examined the intricate piece and compared it to the picture on the box. "Hmm... maybe it's to do with the drawbridge." He pointed at the relevant part in the picture, and Zoe wrinkled her nose. "What's wrong?"

"That part is miles away. I want to use it now."

He laughed. "That's not how it works, sweetheart. You have to construct it in order or it'll collapse. Where will that leave the princess, eh?"

"Homeless," Zara added. "That won't do. Have patience, Zoe. It won't take us long to build it, not now Daddy is helping us."

Hero laughed. "I'm glad you have faith in me."

Zara leaned over and kissed his cheek. "Of course I have faith in you, you're my daddy. You're an expert copper."

"That's debatable, but thanks for the compliment. What we need to

59

find is all the green parts, it'll help to build the base of the castle, agreed?"

The twins nodded, and Zara reached across to collect all the green pieces for Hero to assemble. Half an hour later, Fay called out that dinner was ready. There was still no sign of Louie, who usually ran down the stairs once he heard the word 'dinner'. "You go through to the kitchen; wash your hands first, girls. I'll see what's keeping Louie."

He tore up the stairs. The bathroom door was now open by a couple of inches. He opened it to find the room empty. He tapped on Louie's door, but his son didn't answer. Presuming Louie had his headphones on, listening to loud music, he turned the handle but found it locked. *Damn, what is wrong with him? Why is he deliberately shutting me out like this?*

He banged heavily on the door. "Louie, let me in."

Still no response.

In the end, Hero gave up and went back downstairs, his stomach rumbling at the smell of chips wafting through the house. Fay glanced up from the table.

"No good. I couldn't get him to hear me. Will it keep in the oven?"

"No, I'll reheat it for him later. Leave him alone for now and eat your dinner."

He noticed the way his wife was avoiding eye contact and instinctively knew Louie was the key to why she was upset. *What on earth could be wrong with the lad? He's always been good at sharing any problems he might have.*

Fay looked his way.

He tilted his head and mouthed, "What's going on?"

She shook her head and asked the girls if their dinner was okay.

"Yes, Mummy, it's yummieliscious," Zoe replied, setting both the girls off.

"Good. Eat up, Hero, before it gets cold."

Hero did as his wife suggested, wolfing his evening meal down, hungrier than he had considered himself to be. "Delicious, what's for pudding?" He grinned, trying to make Fay smile a little.

"I picked up a chocolate cheesecake from Tesco earlier, we'll have it with ice cream."

The girls clapped their hands, and their faces lit up.

"I'll give Louie another try." Hero left the table before Fay could stop him. He trekked back upstairs and knocked on his son's door again. "Come on, Louie, open up, son."

He rested his head against the door and waited for the lock to click. Finally, Louie unlocked it and eased the door open, his head bowed low.

"What's up, son? It's not like you to lock yourself in your room like this, or ignore me, come to that."

Louie lifted his head, and Hero couldn't help himself, he gasped and reached for his son, pulling him into a man hug. "My God, who did this to you?"

Louie's dam broke. Hero let him sob and refrained from pestering him for an answer.

"Hush now, you're going to be all right. There, there, son."

Louie eventually pulled back a few paces, his head still low, his chin resting on his chest. "I'll be okay, in time. Thank you."

Hero placed a finger under Louie's chin and raised his head. "Who did this to you, son?"

"I can't, Dad. Please, don't ask. I don't want any further trouble." He wrenched his head away and ran over to the bed.

Hero hesitated. His son clearly wanted some space to deal with what was going on in his head, but the fact that someone had given him a good hiding was clawing at Hero's gut, making him want to retch and bring up his evening meal. "All right. I just want to reassure you that your mother and I are here for you. If you shut yourself away, you're only going to let the vile person who did this to you get away with it. I implore you, don't let that happen, son. They need to be punished."

"You don't understand. They'll come after me again if I open my mouth. I can't say anything. I can't tell you who was involved, Dad. Please don't ask again."

Crushed by his son's pleading words, Hero retreated and paced the landing to cool down then descended the stairs to be with his wife and two daughters, while his son wallowed in his room, distancing himself from those who cared the most about him.

The girls were playing with their Lego again in the lounge. He ruffled their hair as he passed and sought out Fay in the kitchen. She was doing the washing up at the sink. He could tell by the way her shoulders were rising and falling that she was crying.

Hero slipped his arms around her waist and rested his chin against the back of her head. "He'll be fine."

Fay tore the tea towel off the worktop, dried her hands and stared at him. "How do we know that? He's under pressure at school, every teenager is with their schoolwork. Being bullied only adds to his problems."

"I know. We'll see him through this, Fay. You have to have faith, in him, in us as parents."

"I do. But I've also been on the internet, looking up the statistics for teenage suicide attributed to bullying. The figure is atrocious. How are we supposed to combat that if we can't deal with the problem? If he won't allow us to defend his honour, if you like. Oh God, what a frigging awful society we live in. Being at school should be the best years of his life, and here he is, sitting in his room, shutting us and the rest of the world out. Where has my baby gone? The boy I cherish, who once adored his sisters and family life?"

"You're going a bit over the top there."

"Am I? He's locked himself in his room, for fuck's sake. When was the last time, to your knowledge, he did something like that?"

"Never. I agree, this is out of character for him. We're going to need to sit him down and discuss this. See how he wants to proceed. By what he's just told me, I think he wants to brush it under the carpet and forget about it."

"Did he give you any indication why it happened? Who did it? How many there were?"

"No. He refused to discuss it. I'm sure, given space and time, he'll realise his mistake and speak to us. Until then, we're going to have to be patient and give him a wide berth. If we start piling the pressure on, he's likely to retreat into his shell. Who knows what damage that will do in the end? Agreed?"

She turned to face him, her eyes red raw from the scorching tears she'd shed. "I know you're right, but he's my baby. Our baby," she corrected.

"I know. But we have to allow him to make his own decisions on this issue, love. He needs our support not our reprimands for not playing things by the book."

"Okay. I know you're right." She placed a clenched fist to her chest. "My heart is breaking for him."

"Mine is, too, I assure you. I'm looking at this from a male perspective, I promise."

"Meaning I'm too emotionally involved and not seeing things straight, is that it?"

He hugged her tight. "No, that's not what I was saying and you bloody know that. Let's take a back seat for now, let him come to us. I've seen too many families split up over this issue who, with the best intentions, ended up handling the problem in the wrong way from the beginning. I'm desperate not to let that happen to us, sweetheart."

Fay's sobbing started up again, and he clung on tight, a lump of sadness wedging itself in his throat. *Family life sucks at times!* Still, this was the first time they'd been genuinely tested as a family; he hoped it would be the last. "Come on, I promised Sammy a walk after dinner. Why don't we all go out and get some fresh air? I'll see if Louie wants to join us, eh?"

"Okay, maybe it's what we all need right now. I'll finish tidying up, if you get the kids ready. Hopefully, Louie will want to come."

Hero kissed the tip of her nose. "That's the spirit. I love you, Fay. We'll get through this the way we always do, as a family."

"Which reminds me, Cara rang just before you got home. She sounded low and in need of your help."

"Okay. I'll give her a call when we get back. You guys come first, you always will."

"You're a very special man, Hero Nelson."

"I know." He laughed and left the room before she could take a swipe at him. "Get ready, kids, we're going out."

"Where to, Daddy?" the twins asked in unison as they frequently did.

"Never you mind. Tidy up any stray pieces then get your coats and shoes on."

"Okay, Daddy."

The sound of the Lego pieces being thrown back in the box carried upstairs as he ascended them to speak to Louie. He rapped on the door and then pushed it open. Louie was lying on his back on the bed, staring at the ceiling, the curtains drawn, blocking out most of the light.

"Louie, we're going to take Sammy out for a walk, do you want to come with us?"

"No."

"It might do you good to get some fresh air, mate."

"No."

"Are you sure? Your mother and sisters will be disappointed if you don't tag along with us."

"Dad, stop going on. You lot go, I'll be fine where I am. I prefer to stay here, in my room."

"You can't hide in here forever, son."

"I'm not hiding. I just need some space to get my head together."

"All right, then. But Sammy will be disappointed you're not coming with us."

"Sammy is a dog, he doesn't get disappointed."

Behind Hero, Sammy let out a low moan as if he was disputing what Louie had said. "See, he understands perfectly."

Louie shot off the bed and crouched by the door. He opened his arms, and Sammy flew at him. "Sorry, Sammy. Forgive me for shutting you out, I never meant to."

Sammy licked his young master's face and then rested his head on Louie's shoulder. Louie hugged him then glanced up at Hero and smiled through his tears.

"It'll be all right, son. Come on, we'll go as a family, like we always do."

Louie squeezed Sammy one last time and then followed Hero down the stairs. Sammy scooted past them both and began bouncing around at the front door until Hero attached the lead to his collar. "Calm down, boy. The girls have to get ready yet, you know how long they take."

"Come on Zara and Zoe, get a move on," Louie urged his sisters.

Zoe came into the hallway, placed her hands on her hips and glared at her big brother. "You want a matching black eye, Louie?"

Hero fought hard to suppress the snigger bubbling within.

Louie folded his arms and matched his sister's glare. "Yeah, and who's going to give me one?"

"Ooo... tough boy," Zoe replied, and then burst into laughter.

Louie cracked a smile as well.

Five minutes later, they left the house and took a leisurely stroll to the park. Louie held Sammy's lead and remained at the back of the pack. The girls nattered on as usual, there was never a lull in conversation with those two around. Hero held Fay's hand; all was good in the world, again.

They entered the park and headed towards the children's adventure area. Hero turned around when he heard Sammy whining to see Louie had stopped and was staring at a group of boys sitting on the equipment in the adventure area. He also noted how the other children kept their distance from the five lads. He took a few steps back and said, "Do you know those boys, son?"

Louie gulped. "They're trouble, Dad. Can we go elsewhere?"

"Were they the ones?" Hero took in the five boys' appearances in case he'd need to identify them at a later date.

"I don't want to talk about it. You go ahead, I'll go home." Louie handed Hero Sammy's lead and raced out of the park.

Hero didn't call after him. Instead, he watched the boys' reaction to seeing Louie run off. They all started laughing and high-fiving each other. His blood seared his veins until the heat rose in his cheeks.

Fay slipped an arm through his to gain his attention. "I take it they're the ones. What are you going to do?"

"Nothing. I've made a note of them. I don't recognise any of them, do you?"

"I've seen one or two around the estate close to us but I can't tell you their names. Poor Louie. We should go after him."

"Yeah, I agree. Come on, girls. Let's go."

"But, Daddy, we've only just got here," Zara complained.

"And now it's time to go. This was all about giving Sammy a walk, remember?"

That statement was enough to deter the twins from complaining further. The girls ran ahead of Hero and Fay.

He passed the lead over to Fay to hold. "Would you mind? I might as well ring Cara on the way back."

"Good idea. She'll be thinking you're ignoring her."

"Problems, problems. I hope she's all right."

"Only one way of finding out. I'll leave you to it and walk with the girls, keep them occupied, give you some space."

He kissed her and smiled. She walked on ahead with the twins. Hero glanced over his shoulder to see the five boys all standing in a group, staring at him. He was sorely tempted to march over to them and give them a piece of his mind but thought better of it. It was never best to tackle a problem when you're riled up. For a few more seconds, he stared at the lad he perceived to be the leader, who was standing proud of the group, then he took out his phone to call his sister and turned his back on the boys.

"Hey, you. Sorry for the delay, the girls needed a hand, and then dinner got in the way, you know how it is. How are you diddling?"

"Hi, thanks for getting back to me. I'm fine, sort of. No, I'm not. I'm low and I fear only you will understand."

"Oh, sweetie. I'm sorry to hear that. Is it because of the baby?"

"Come right out and ask, why don't you?"

He grimaced. "Sorry, insensitive bugger, you know what I'm like. I don't know what else I can say on the subject. You know Fay and I are always here for you."

"I know. But my therapist says it's good to talk when you're feeling overwhelmed."

"Damn, and is that how you feel at the moment? Want me to come over and be with you?"

"Yes, but no, it's getting late now. You spend time with your family, I'll be all right. I wanted to hear your voice, that's all."

"Why don't you come and stay with us for a few days?" *Damn, what am I saying? With all that's going on with Louie at the moment!*

"No, it's okay. I'd rather stay here. I'm binge-watching *Game of Thrones.*"

"You are? That's the third time, isn't it? Don't you find it depressing to watch?"

"No, not at all. There are light-hearted moments thrown into the mix now and again."

"I can't remember discovering many of those. Why don't you binge-watch *Only Fools and Horses* or something along those lines instead? It'll be better for your soul."

"Nah, blood and gore, that's me. Within reason anyway. What are you guys up to at the moment?"

"Same old. We're out for a walk with Sammy. Heading back home now. Fay and the girls are walking on ahead so I can talk to you."

"Where's Louie?"

"He was with us. He turned back a while ago, got some urgent homework he needs to finish before the morning."

"Ah, I see. He's a good lad. He's going to do well at school, I can tell. Unlike you."

"Hey, thanks for that. No, you've always been the twin with the extra brain cells on board."

They both laughed. It was good to hear her sound happier, he'd done his job. "Why don't you come round at the weekend? We'll try and do something special with the kids."

"I'd love to go to that adventure theme park again."

"That's a date then, come round at about eleven on Saturday. We'll take a picnic with us."

"Just what the doctor ordered to put a smile on my face. Thanks for giving me something to look forward to, bro."

"You're welcome. Keep that chin high, sis. I hate it when you're down."

"I know. I'm trying to do my best, honest. See you Saturday, thanks for calling me back."

"Love you lots."

"Right backatcha."

Hero ended the call and caught up with his family once more. He took Sammy's leash from Fay and hooked an arm around her waist. The girls were chuntering on about what they'd been drawing at school. Hero's thoughts lay with his son and the group of boys back at the park. How he had wanted to intervene. To pull the boys into the station, to scare the shit out of them. That would have marked their cards for them. Hopefully, deter them from picking on boys smaller than themselves. He was aware how these things escalated quickly. What started out as simple bullying at school could easily turn into far more serious crimes as the group formed a terrifying gang, such as the Krull Gang, the one Hero had dealt with a few years back. Monsters they were, there was no other name for them.

He'd been the happiest he'd ever been when he'd wrapped up that case. Manchester was a safer city by far, since their departure.

5

"*I*'m on my way. Stop hounding me, I'll be with you shortly."
Lizzie laughed and replaced her mobile in her handbag. She
was always one for running late, it drove her friends, Jo and Laura,
nuts. They had arranged to meet up at eight, and it was already ten
past. She upped her pace, as much as she could manage in her strappy
high-heeled sandals. She regretted not wearing her trainers, she could
have changed into her sandals later. *Hindsight is a wonderful thing.*
She looked left then right as she crossed the road. Not far now. *I
wonder what we're going to choose to eat tonight. I fancy a Chinese
meal, haven't had one for a...*

Lizzie was so lost in thought that she neglected to hear or see the
van pull up alongside her. Two sets of arms grabbed her and dragged
her into the vehicle. One of the men placed a hand over her mouth. She
bit him, earning a thump in the face. She heard the crunch of bones and
instantly knew that her nose was broken. The pain was intense. *Shit!
What's happening to me? Where are they taking me? I knew I should
have worn my damned trainers, I could have outrun these bastards.* In
school, she'd been the fastest girl on the track. Her teacher had begged
her to take up the sport at county level, but her love of being with

friends, socialising and going out with boys had won the battle in the end. *Yeah, and look where that's got me now.*

"Tie her up. She's a feisty one, I can tell. Someone slap something over her nose. I don't want any blood in my van, got that?" the driver shouted over his shoulder.

The two guys in the back searched the area and eventually found an oily rag which one of them shoved over Lizzie's nose. She thrashed her head from side to side, trying to avoid coming into contact with the filthy piece of cloth. She failed. A hand bashed her injured nose, making her yelp.

"Don't, please. It hurts. Why are you doing this?" she asked, her gaze swivelling between the two men sitting across from her.

The one holding the cloth to her nose changed positions and sat next to her. "Keep your mouth shut and…"

"And what?" she demanded. Her pulse rate had surged, hitting the max. It was affecting her ability to breathe properly through the oily fumes on the rag. She twisted her head, but her aggressor held firm, hurting her even more.

"Please, I can't breathe properly."

"Good, stop struggling then."

She did as she was told, her panic ebbing and flowing at regular intervals. Lizzie peered through the windscreen. They were approaching the point where she was due to meet Jo and Laura. *Oh God, there they are. Please drive past them, don't stop. Leave them out of this. Whatever this is.*

Thankfully, the driver whizzed past her friends. Tears bulged as she saw their pissed-off faces. She wondered if she'd ever see them again after what was about to happen to her. Who were these men, and what did they want from her? She tried to keep her thoughts away from the obvious conclusion. She was scared. The farther they travelled, the more scared she became. It was still relatively light outside, so she could see where they were going. Out of the city. Where, though?

Unimaginable thoughts stirred in her mind. She fought the urge to be sick, aware that she could possibly choke on her own vomit, judging by the force with which the man was holding the disgusting cloth against her mouth. *God, please help me. I didn't mean to fall out with my sister for taking my ideal job from me. I'd happily forgive her if it meant you getting these men to set me free. Please, don't let them hurt me any more than they have done already. Please. I need help, please supply it. I promise I'll start attending church regularly, if that'll persuade you to intervene. Please, someone help me.*

A woodland appeared ahead of them. The driver indicated and pulled over in front of a large clump of trees. "Okay, let's get her out. Grab the rope, Barry. Todd, keep a tight hold of her, she's bound to try and make a run for it once she's out of the van."

"I won't, I promise," Lizzie's response was suppressed by the cloth.

"Get out, bitch. Any funny business and we'll go after your family, got that?" the thug manhandling her warned.

"Yes, okay. You have my word. Please, don't hurt me. I have a little bit of savings in the bank, if that will help. Less than five hundred, but I can get more. I'll need time to do that, but it's not impossible. Please, don't hurt me."

"Shut that fucking mouth of yours or I'll bust your nose again."

"I'm sorry. Okay, I'll shut up."

The guy shook her and got in her face. He snarled, his eyes increasing in size, his stare intensifying. "Shut the fuck up, that's your final warning. Right?"

She nodded, gently because of the way he was still suppressing her nose and mouth with the cloth. He forced her to walk towards the three other men waiting ahead of them. One of them, the other one who had been sitting opposite her in the back of the van, was swinging a rope back and forth in his right hand. It had a noose around the end. She closed her eyes, blocking out the image, and prayed for someone to come to her rescue if God had chosen to ignore her plea. *Someone please help me. Please, don't let them kill me. I'm far too young to die. Please.*

"Okay, time to have some fun with the bitch," the leader of the group announced, malice evident in his tone. He removed the rag from her mouth.

Lizzie's eyes shot open. She shook her head and trembled all over. "Please, don't do this. Leave me here. I promise I won't call the police."

The leader took a step into her personal space. "Too right you won't call the police because you'll be *dead*."

Lizzie opened her mouth to scream, but no noise came out; her saliva had dried up as the shock set in. *Is this really how my life will end? With these bastards having their way with me before they kill me?* Terrifying thoughts whirled in her mind as if they were being shunted around a pinball machine.

Rip! Her jacket and blouse were torn from her upper half and left hanging, draping over her short skirt, by the man in charge. An evil smirk twitched at his mouth, pulling it apart to reveal teeth that were overlapped in several places.

Her heart was pounding that hard she struggled to breathe. Unable to take any more, she passed out.

"*J*esus, wake her up. Get some water from the van, she needs to be awake for what we have in store for her."

"Come on, man. You can see how terrified she was. Just do what you have to do and let's get out of here," Mick said.

Daz pounced on him. Jabbed his brother in the chest and shouted, "Hey, shit for frigging brains, I'm in charge around here, got that? You had your opportunity to take the reins and you refused it. So don't start fucking trying to pull a fast one on me now, got that?"

His brother struck out, knocking Daz's hand away. "Yeah, you're in charge. Do what you want, man, you always do anyway, so what's bloody new?" Mick marched back to the van, yanked open the door and slid into the passenger seat.

"Ignore him. It must be his time of the month, or his missus', and that's what's pissing him off." Daz laughed and turned his attention to the girl again. "Barry, grab the water from the van. Make it snappy."

Barry reached the van in six strides on his extra-long legs. He returned and handed the bottle to Daz. He undid the lid and squirted the large bottle in the girl's face. She spluttered as the water hit her and went up her injured nose. She stared up at the three men, fear resonating quickly once she remembered where she was and what was about to happen to her. "Please, leave me alone. Don't do this."

Daz leaned down, clutched a clump of her hair and yanked her to her feet. "Don't fucking tell me what to do, bitch."

"I'm sorry, I didn't mean to do that."

He motioned for the other two men to hold her while he removed the rest of her clothes, leaving her naked in the chilled air. She trembled under his scrutinising gaze, gulping now and then.

"Who wants to be first this time?" he asked the others.

"I don't mind," Barry piped up.

Daz took his place, holding the woman's right arm while Barry unzipped his trousers. Daz glanced at her; she had closed her eyes, squeezing them tightly shut.

He laughed. "I don't think she's keen on you sticking Mr Rod in her, mate."

"Tough, right? Here goes."

Ten minutes later, all three of them had finished raping her. She was a mess, sobbing so hard the bloodied snot was running freely from her nose. Daz smiled smugly, loving what he was seeing. He picked up the noose and placed it around her slim throat.

"Please…" she whispered, no longer able to fight the inevitable.

"If you insist." Daz threw the other end of the rope into the tree and hoisted the woman off the ground.

6

$\mathcal{R}$ay Dillon, the desk sergeant at the station, was waiting for Hero to arrive at work the following morning. He held the main door open for him. This was unusual for Ray.

The gesture tightened Hero's gut. "All right, Ray?"

"Not really, sir. I've just got in. I was looking through the notes left by the desk sergeant from the night shift, and something struck me as odd."

Hero's eyes narrowed. "In what way?" He entered the building, and Ray picked up a set of notes from the counter and showed them to Hero.

"As you can see, these two ladies were waiting for their good friend to appear last night so they could go into town together, but she stood them up."

Hero shrugged and scanned the rest of the notes. "Maybe she had a better offer."

Ray shook his head. "Not in her to do that, sir. They rang her phone over and over, she never picked up. Again, that behaviour isn't normal for this young lady."

"All right, you've ground me down. I'll visit the girls, see what they can tell us. Anything suspicious reported overnight to correspond with this?"

"First thing I did was check the incidents reported overnight—nothing out of the ordinary there, sir. Definitely nothing pertaining to what these two young ladies reported, anyway."

"Okay. I'll wait for Julie to arrive and then shoot over there."

"She's at her desk already."

"Right. In other words, you deem this urgent enough for me to forego my morning coffee and daily ritual of scrabbling around my desk going through the onerous chore of dealing with the post."

Ray smiled briefly and picked up the phone. "Yes, sir. Call it a hunch."

"That's good enough for me. Tell Julie I'll be waiting in the car."

"On it now, sir."

Hero strolled back to the car and sat in the driver's seat, drumming his fingers on the steering wheel until his partner emerged from the building and rushed to join him.

"Well, that was a turn up for the books, you not coming into work like that." Julie slotted her belt into the clasp.

With the engine already running, Hero pulled away from his parking space and said, "I didn't see the point in traipsing upstairs to fetch you, why waste my energy?"

Julie grunted. "Ray said something about a woman going missing, is that where we're going?"

"Sort of. We need to interview the woman's two friends. They were expecting her to join them last night for a meal and drinks and she never showed up."

"Possibly had a better offer?"

"First thing that came to my mind; the desk sergeant thought it was unlikely. The girls were freaking out about their friend. They've been calling her mobile constantly, and she hasn't picked up. Again, that's unusual for her."

"Okay, you've convinced me. So you're going to see the girls because you believe this could be linked to the new investigation?"

Hero quickly glanced at his partner. "Don't you?" He turned his attention back to the road ahead.

"Hard to say on what you've just told me."

"Which is why I felt it was imperative that we should see these ladies ASAP."

"Where are we heading?" Julie fiddled with her confounded mobile, trying to be discreet about it but failing.

"They both work in the city, one at a hairdresser's and the other at a betting shop."

The car fell silent while Julie scrolled through her phone. Hero seethed but bit down on his tongue rather than have the usual argument with his partner first thing in the morning.

He parked the car in a spot across the street from the hairdresser's and went in search of Joanne Tomlinson. Hero pushed the door open to the swish salon and walked up to the girl standing behind the reception desk. The staff were all dressed alike, in a bubble-gum pink uniform. He flashed his warrant card. "DI Nelson and DS Shaw, is the owner or your boss around?"

"Oh, right, the police. Yes, Mrs Dyer's out the back. I'll get her for you." She left her desk and returned with a smartly dressed woman in her early fifties. Her thick-rimmed glasses had been thrust through her rich curly auburn hair, and a cautious smile pinched at her lips.

"Can I help? I'm Felicity Dyer. I own this establishment."

"We hope so. We're here to speak to Joanne Tomlinson, if she's free?"

The woman raised an eyebrow and peered over her right shoulder at several of the stylists tending to their customers. "She's in the middle of a cut and blow-dry by the look of it. Can't this wait? This is a busy salon, and if the girls slip behind it'll give us a bad reputation."

We wouldn't want that, would we, love? "I'm sorry, it can't."

She heaved out a sigh. "Just a minute, I'll have a word with her."

"Thank you." Hero issued one of his more dazzling smiles, trying to break down the woman's tough exterior, sensing she had a hidden softness to her nature.

She returned and motioned for them to take a seat. "She's going to be five minutes. Joanne then has five minutes to clean up her station before her next client appears. I'd be grateful if you allowed her to keep to her strict schedule. We've had enough bad reviews about time-keeping to last us a lifetime."

"Don't worry, we won't keep her long, I promise. If it wasn't important, we wouldn't be here, I can assure you."

"Yes, yes. I'll leave you to it." She turned to walk away but whispered in the receptionist's ear as she passed.

"Friendly sort," Hero commented, taking a seat by the window. He tapped his knee which was twitching up and down while they waited the five minutes until Joanne was free.

Finally, the young woman led her customer to the reception area, removed her protective cape and helped the woman with her fur-edged coat. Which Hero felt was a tad over the top, given that it was supposed to be summer, although looking outside, he was forced to admit that it was chillier than normal today.

The receptionist pointed at Hero and Julie. Joanne smiled and joined them. She lowered her voice. "I've only got a few minutes. Want to talk here or somewhere more private? Such as the staffroom."

"I think the staffroom would be best. I'd prefer not to distract the rest of your colleagues."

"Very wise. Felicity is a fierce boss, I can tell you. Come with me." She led them into a windowless room which housed a bank of lockers and a sink. On the draining board were a kettle and a tray of mugs, and underneath the sink was a fridge. All pretty basic, considering how plush the salon appeared to be.

"Nice," Hero said.

Joanne giggled. "Not the word I would choose to describe this place. Can we get on with it?"

"Of course."

The three of them sat around a small circular table.

Joanne gripped her hands together tightly. "You're here about Lizzie, aren't you?"

"That's right. I'll get to the point because we have limited time. You rang the station to report her missing, is that correct?"

"Yes, Laura and I were due to meet her to go into town last night for drinks and something to eat. She didn't show up. She's usually late; we were due to meet at eight. By the time eight-thirty came around we were freaking out, sensed that something was wrong, so we called nine-nine-nine and were told that you guys couldn't do anything until twenty-four hours had passed. That's a ridiculous rule, isn't it?"

"Sometimes. Saying that, if someone shows up after only a few hours of going missing it can save us a lot of time and effort, let alone resources."

"Ah, yes, okay, I can understand that. Either way, we know Lizzie, she wouldn't go missing like this. Therefore, I believe something is wrong. I dread to think what that might be. Will you help us find her?"

"We're going to do our very best, but we need more details from you."

"Such as? I've told you all I know."

"Lizzie's address. Which route she usually takes into town. Does she have a car? Or was she using public transport? That sort of thing."

Julie withdrew her notebook and poised her pen.

"Her address is fifty-two Hinchbottom Road. She doesn't have a car, refuses to use public transport, either that or she prefers to walk to keep fit. I keep telling her to jump into a taxi rather than amble into town, for this very reason."

"Is that caution speaking or do you have a reason for believing your friend might not be safe walking into town?"

"Er, hello! You only have to listen to the news to know how safe it is out there for women these days."

Hero nodded, reflecting on the recent case, down south, of the young woman whose life had been taken by a police officer. "Okay, I understand what you're saying, and yet, despite your warnings, she still chose to walk into town. Are you sure that's what happened last night?"

"Pretty sure. She's one of these types who stick to a routine where at all possible. She usually walks into town, especially when the nights are lighter."

"Okay, which route does she generally take?"

"She tends to walk down Hyde Road. We were due to meet at the Tesco Express near the bottom."

"Is there anything else you can tell us? Does she have a regular boyfriend?"

"No. We're all single. We've had our fair share of heartbreak over the years and made a pact to steer clear of men for the time being."

"Did she have anyone interested in her?"

Joanne frowned and contemplated the question for a moment then shook her head. "No, not that she told us about. You think someone she knows has been stalking her, is that it?"

Hero raised a hand. "Let's not get carried away here. It was only a question. What about past boyfriends, are any of them likely to have pestered her, perhaps?"

"No, none that I can think of. She's only had one serious boyfriend in the last few years. He moved down south and is married to someone he met at work, so Lizzie said."

"Okay, that helps. What about work, where does she work?"

"She works for an estate agency as a secretary. It's only up the road. Sometimes we meet up for lunch."

"Have you rung them this morning to see if she's shown up for work?"

Joanne hung her head. "Sorry, it's been full-on since I got in this morning. I had every intention of ringing them, but it slipped my mind when Felicity started bending my ear about keeping to schedule today."

"No need to apologise. She seems a very demanding boss."

"You don't know the half of it. If we slip behind on our appointments, she docks our wages." She gasped and looked at the clock on the wall. "Which reminds me, I'd better get a shift on. Sorry I couldn't be much help. Are you going to see Laura now?"

"Yes, there's no need for you to apologise. I think we have enough to go on to get us started. Thanks for sparing the time to chat with us."

Joanne led the way back into the salon. Her boss was standing by her office door, tapping the gold watch on her wrist.

"Just finished. Getting back to work now, boss."

"Good. I don't have to tell you how important Mrs Gillespie is to this salon, do I?"

"No, you don't. I'll get cleaned up, ready for her arrival."

Hero and Julie bid Joanne farewell, leaving her to tend to her strict responsibilities before the next appointment arrived.

"Are we going to see Laura next or call at Lizzie's place of work?" Julie asked, looking up at the dark sky overhead.

"I think Laura will probably tell us the same as Joanne, so let's go to the estate agency instead. It can't harm."

They set off, the streets bustling as life began to get back to near normal after the pandemic that had blighted the world, and arrived at the offices of Homes for You within a few minutes just as the heavens opened.

"Lucky escape," Julie muttered, following Hero through the front door.

He showed his ID to the first person they came to, a young woman with an infectious smile. "Hello there. Ghastly weather by the look of things, how can I help?"

"Typical of Manchester. We get used to it. We were hoping to have a word with your boss."

"I can see if Stuart is available. Care to take a seat? I won't be long."

Instead of sitting, Hero strolled over to the house particulars on display this side of the window.

"Not thinking of moving, are you?" Julie whispered behind him.

"It's often on my mind. Our place can feel a tad small at times, and the twins are growing up fast, they'll probably be demanding separate rooms soon."

"As girls do," Julie noted. "Where would be your ideal location if the need arose?"

"I haven't really thought about it. I suppose staying close to the centre and work would be preferable, but the closer you get to the city, the higher the council tax, true?"

"Yeah. Rob and I like where we live. Not too far to travel but still far enough out of town for us to regard it being rural."

"Do you tend to do much at the weekends?"

"We go for walks in the countryside, weather permitting. That's when time allows, you know, after the housework and other chores have been completed. There's always something to be done around the house, isn't there?"

Hero rolled his eyes. "Tell me about it. Does Rob help with the chores?"

"He does, actually. We both work long hours. He understands what it takes to run a house and chips in quite often. I bet you're the same, what with Fay working full-time as well."

He cleared his throat, ashamed to admit that he didn't tend to do that much around the house, not compared to Fay. Something he would need to look at over the coming months. The last thing he wanted to do was to take Fay for granted, which by the sounds of what Julie had just said, was a distinct possibility.

"You wanted to see me? I'm Stuart Lockhart, I own this place."

Hero turned to face the man in his forties, wearing a pinstripe navy suit and a jazzy-coloured tie. He produced his ID. "DI Nelson and DS Shaw. Would it be possible for us to speak in private, Mr Lockhart?"

"Of course. I do hope we haven't broken the law at all, Inspector?"

"Not as far as we know. It's just a general enquiry."

He showed them through to a large office just off the main reception area. "Take a seat."

Julie and Hero sat opposite him. Lockhart picked up a pen and started rolling it through his fingers. "What can I do for you?"

"We're here about a member of your staff."

Lockhart frowned. "You are? Who might that be?"

"Lizzie Watts. Has she shown up for work today?"

"No. I'm disappointed she hasn't rung in with an excuse either. What's she been up to?"

"She was supposed to have met up with two friends last night but didn't show up. They were concerned about her and reported Lizzie as missing."

"Oh heck. And is she? Missing?"

"We've yet to establish that. Would you mind telling us what type of character she is at work?"

"Character? Like the others, I suppose. I believe I'm a fair boss, they all enjoy their time at work. I'm not a tyrant. If she'd wanted time off, all she had to do was ask and I would have given it to her. I don't appreciate being kept in the dark about things, though. However, if you say she's gone missing then I have to say I'm concerned about her, this is totally unlike Lizzie. She's a responsible member of this firm, one I can usually rely on. Why do you think she's gone missing?"

"That's what we're trying to find out, sir. Does she have much contact with the general public?"

"No, not at all. She works out the back most of the time, alongside me. My right-hand woman, if you like."

"You'd be fairly close to her in that case? Close enough for her to confide in you if anything in her personal life was amiss?"

"I suppose so. She hasn't said anything along those lines to me, not recently, not that I can recall. Are you treating her disappearance as suspicious?"

"Yes, I think we have to, given the information we've obtained regarding her character."

"Oh my. And here was me cursing her when she didn't show up this morning. What a shit boss I am."

"Please, don't go blaming yourself. I'm sure many of us would have reacted the same way if we felt a member of staff had let us down."

"She's generally reliable. I should have realised something was wrong rather than slating her for not showing up."

"Don't worry. Would you mind asking around your staff for us? Maybe she's contacted one of them today."

He shook his head. "Already done it. I asked them earlier this morning when I thought she wasn't going to show up. I tried her house phone and mobile number, but they just rang out. That's a lie, the mobile went to voicemail. I left a heated message which I regret leaving now, in the circumstances."

"It was a tough call, I appreciate that. Okay, we'll leave you to it then." Hero rose from his seat. It was a waste of time them being there, that much was obvious.

"Please find her. I dread to think what's happened to her if she's gone missing. Do people truly go missing just for the sake of it?"

"Not in our experience. Thanks for your help. Hopefully, she'll show up soon."

He led them to the front door, his steps faltering a little. "It's hard to believe. I can't get my head around it. If something has happened to her, I'll never forgive myself for leaving that distasteful message on her phone."

Hero winced, feeling sorry for the man. *The trouble is, most of us shout the odds before we truly know what's going on in someone's life. You're the prime example, matey.* "Thanks for your assistance."

He closed the door behind them. "I can imagine what was said in that message, can't you?" Julie mumbled.

"Yeah, if she ends up dead, he'll reflect on that message till the day he dies. Might deter him from flinging shit next time."

"Off to see Laura now?"

"Yep, I bet it will prove to be a waste of our time."

Hero was right. Laura was in tears throughout the interview, fearing something bad had happened to her best friend. She couldn't tell them anything more than Joanne had already told them about the night before, so Julie and Hero left before the doom and gloom sank into their bones. The only positive thing Laura managed to do was supply them with an up-to-date image of Lizzie from her phone.

They were on their way back to the station when a call came over the radio that a body had been found in Craven Woods on the outskirts of town. Hero and Julie glanced at each other. Hero nodded, instructing Julie to respond to the call. He flicked the switch, and they conducted the journey under the siren. An ominous feeling of dread worked its way through Hero's body. He inhaled and exhaled at regular intervals to calm his nerves.

"You think it's her, don't you?" Julie said when they were a short distance away from the location.

"Maybe. I hate speculating, and let's be fair, we don't know if the body is male or female yet, do we?"

"True. They usually tell us. I wonder why they haven't bothered to divulge that this time."

"We're about to find out. Gerrard is here, which is always a positive in my eyes."

"He's a good man," Julie agreed.

After stepping out of the vehicle and slipping into their suits, Hero and Julie stopped at the cordon to sign the Crime Scene Log, then they ducked under the tape and travelled a few more feet into the woods to find Gerrard. He was staring down at the charred remains of a body.

"Jesus, you're kidding me!" Hero exclaimed, his hand instinctively covering his mouth to prevent him from vomiting.

"It ain't pretty, Hero. We found the body here, but I suspect she was hanging from the tree before someone set her alight."

"Fuck it! You said *she*, are you sure?"

"As sure as I can be at this stage. I won't state the obvious, tell you how I know."

"Oh, right, that told me. We've been investigating the disappearance of a young woman. A Lizzie Watts, she went missing last night. I'm wondering if this could be her."

"Possibly. I haven't stumbled across any ID or mobile for the victim as yet."

Hero requested to see Julie's phone. She opened it at the photo of Lizzie they'd obtained from the sobbing Laura, barely half an hour before.

"I'm not sure why you're bothering to make a comparison, Hero." Gerrard's brow wrinkled.

"Yeah, neither am I, bloody daft idea. There, I've said it, there's no need for you to tell me. I don't suppose you'll be able to tell me if she suffered before her death. No, let me rephrase that, do you think she was set alight pre- or post-mortem?"

"You're right, there's no point in you asking such a silly question, I can't possibly know the facts of the crime until I've opened her up."

"But you can hazard a guess, yes?"

"Not going to happen, not in this case. The remains are too far gone for me to speculate."

"It was just a suggestion, more out of hope than expectation. I thank you for your candour. Anything else you can tell us about the crime?"

"Nothing worthwhile as yet, sorry. You know what it's like when dealing with fire."

"I do." Hero studied the smouldering remains of the victim and the soil around her body. "What's that?"

"Ah, you spotted it, I wondered if you would," Gerrard replied with a grin.

"Well? No, wait, is that something around her neck?" Against his better judgement, he crouched to get a closer look at the victim.

"Yes, that's why I initially stated that she has likely been hung from the tree above. The branch probably gave way during the fire and then disintegrated. I took a gander under the body and discovered charred wood. That's the conclusion I'm going with anyway."

"What's the alternative? That she was barbecued?"

Julie retched beside him. "The images you guys are flinging around are turning my stomach."

"And that's not?" Hero pointed at the victim.

Julie huffed and walked away.

"Hey, don't go storming off. I need you to get on to the station. We need to find a next of kin. Better still, can you ring either Joanne or Laura?"

"Crap, what shall I tell them if they ask why we need the information?"

Hero puffed out his cheeks and tutted. "Use your imagination, partner."

"But what if it's not her?" she retorted tartly.

"She has a point," Gerrard added.

"All right. Just say you're tying up loose ends, we missed a trick, or that we should have got the details from them at the time they were interviewed, how's that?"

"It'll do. I'm on it now."

Hero nodded then glanced at Gerrard. "When are we likely to get an identification?"

"Could be a few days. If you have a victim in mind and you track down the next of kin, we'll be able to ascertain who the victim is if we can get hold of their dental records. Without them, we're screwed, unless you can supply any other form of DNA for comparison purposes."

"I hear you. Let's see what Julie comes up with. Shit, why is nothing cut and dried? More to the point, who in their right bloody mind would set a woman on fire and why?"

"Beggars belief, doesn't it?" Gerrard scratched the side of his head with his gloved hand. "If it is the girl in the picture, what a bloody waste of a young life. What do you know about her?"

"Enough to know that she was young, free and single, and enjoying life. No reason for her to get involved with someone capable of committing such a crime—she was sworn off men, according to her friends. She was on her way to meet them. My suggestion is someone possibly abducted her en route. What else they subjected her to, well, I really don't want to think about that, the outcome was bad enough as it is to consider."

"Despicable, I agree. Poor woman. Still, we can't stand around here gossiping, I need to get her transferred back to the lab."

"Don't let me stop you. We'll get on with the investigation."

"Are you linking the two you're working on?" Gerrard snapped his glove at the wrist.

"I think we should, don't you? Two gruesome crimes within what? Twenty-four to thirty-six hours. Let's hope the killer isn't on some kind of spree."

"Yeah, for all our sakes. And yes, I would be inclined to link the crimes at this stage, I think it would be the wrong decision not to."

"Ring me when you get a result."

"I'll need you to supply the information we discussed before I can get started."

"I'll keep on top of Julie."

Gerrard raised an eyebrow.

Hero shook his head in disgust. "Bugger, get your mind out of the gutter. Fay would string me up. Ouch, no pun intended."

"Get out of here, before you put your size tens in any more shit pats."

"I'm gone." Hero waved and joined Julie at the car. "Any luck?"

"Joanne told me that Lizzie's parents are divorced, her mother is a nurse at Christie's."

"The cancer hospital?"

"That's right. Want me to give them a ring, see if she's on duty today?"

"Get in. Yes, do that, I'll head out that way, just in case she is. Damn, this is going to be a tough one."

"They all are," Julie admitted, getting into the car beside him.

Hero knew the hospital well. His cousin had leukaemia as a child and had been a frequent patient right up until he'd sadly passed away at the age of only fourteen. Hero's parents had tried to protect him rather than tell him the truth about Tristan's passing, but it hadn't taken him long to figure it out for himself. He'd come over all cold the morning Tristan had slipped away, it was obvious something was wrong. Cara had felt the same way that morning, she confessed as much when they'd met up that evening. They were in tune, as most twins are. They had both mourned the loss of Tristan by holding a midnight vigil for him. It had helped them cope with the devastating loss. Tristan had been ill, in and out of Christie's most of his young life. He'd been diagnosed at the age of four.

"Are you all right?" Julie asked.

"Sorry, I drifted off there for a few moments. Going back to the hospital where my cousin died is going to affect me."

"Sorry, I had no idea. Was he very young?"

"Yes, fourteen."

"How dreadful, I'm sorry you had to deal with that."

"All good, it was years ago. I haven't visited the hospital since, thank goodness, no real need to."

"Anyway, Jane Watts is on duty until seven this evening."

. . .

*T*hey drew into the short-stay car park, and Hero collected the ticket to pay on the way out. Sitting at the reception desk was a friendly older woman with grey hair.

"Hello there, how may I help?"

Hero produced his warrant card. "DI Nelson and DS Shaw. We were wondering if it would be possible to speak with a colleague of yours, a Jane Watts."

"I can ask her to come and see you, if you'd care to wait over there." She pointed at the group of chairs behind them.

"Thanks, that would be brilliant."

They stood to one side as the woman placed the call. "She'll be with you in five minutes."

"Thanks," Hero replied. He paced the floor.

"Do you have to do that? You're making me nervous," his partner complained.

"Sorry. I'm feeling a little anxious about this. We don't know how she's likely to react, do we? Should we even be here?"

"It's a difficult one. Gerrard needs her dental records or a DNA sample to make the ID."

"I know, but what if it's not her and I'm about to cause this woman untold worry?"

Julie sat in one of the chairs and flicked through a magazine. "There's no other way around it."

Hero paced the floor, widening his circle at times until a woman showed up and spoke to the receptionist. She came towards them. Hero noticed her name tag and gulped.

"Hi, I'm Jane Watts, you wanted to see me? I have to tell you I'm a little nervous, I've never received a visit from the police before. Did I run a red light or something? On my way down here I've tried to think what I might have done wrong but I'm struggling to come up with anything."

Hero smiled and produced his ID again. "DI Nelson. There's no need for you to be worried, Mrs Watts, we appreciate you coming to speak with us. We won't keep you long. Is there somewhere we can go for a private chat?"

"Wait, I'll see what Gail can suggest." She nipped back to the receptionist who pointed to a room behind them, close to the entrance. "Yes, Gail said the consultation room over here is free, will that do?"

"Sounds perfect." He and Julie followed Mrs Watts into the bog-standard square room that was filled with a rack of pamphlets and a small table with two chairs.

"Shall I fetch another chair?"

Hero shook his head. "You two ladies can take a seat, I'll stand, it's no problem."

She sat at the desk and put her hands in her lap. "Please, don't keep me in suspense any longer."

"I won't. This isn't easy for me to say, but when was the last time you contacted your daughter?"

"A couple of days ago, why?" She sat forward and placed her clenched hands on the table.

Hero sighed. "She was reported missing last night by two of her friends, Joanne and Laura, do you know them?"

"Yes, of course I know them. My God, what are you telling me? Is my daughter okay?" Her eyes sparkled with unshed tears, and the high colour she'd had in her cheeks when she'd arrived quickly dispersed.

Hero's heart rate escalated to another level. "The truth is, we don't know. A body was found in the woods earlier..." He paused when she gasped and gripped the edge of the desk. "Are you all right? Can I get you a glass of water?"

"Yes, please. I have angina, I keep it under control with medication."

Hero shot out of the room and picked up a paper cup at the dispenser. He filled it with water and charged back into the room and handed it to the nurse. "What about your medication, can I get it for you?"

"No. It's in my locker. I'll get it soon. Go on, you were saying?"

"This morning we found a body in the woods."

"Is it her?" she whispered before downing the water.

"We're unsure. I'm sorry to have to tell you that if the body is that of your daughter, we're going to need another form of identification for her."

"What are you saying? I can't get my head around this. Where is my daughter?"

"This is so hard. The body found in the woods was unrecognisable, do you understand?"

She shook her head, and the tears fell onto her cheeks. Her knuckles turned white the more she gripped the table. "Please, don't tell me that. I can't believe I'm hearing this. My beautiful Lizzie, are you sure it's her? It could be anyone, couldn't it? Someone else's child, instead of mine."

"It could, that's true. We're going to need to identify the victim from their dental records. For that to happen, we're going to need your authority for us to approach the dentist."

"Of course. If there's no way around this. I can't believe she was reported missing but no one bothered to inform me."

"I'm sorry. Not wishing to make apologies for the girls, I think they may have thought they were doing the right thing, keeping you out of the loop, under the circumstances."

"I had, have, a right to know if something is wrong with my daughter. Her dentist is in Manchester. I'll know it as soon as I see the name. I can't think of them off the top of my head." Julie looked up the dentists in the area and handed Mrs Watts the phone. She jabbed her finger at one halfway down the list. "That's it. Simpson, that's the one." She gave the phone back to Julie, but her gaze remained on Hero. "What are you going to do about this?"

"We'll go and have a word with the dentist in person, put him in touch with the pathologist who is carrying out the post-mortem."

Mrs Watts covered her face with her hands. "I refuse to think this is her. Am I allowed to do that?"

"Of course you are. I'm sorry to have broken the news to you like this. It's the part of the job I detest the most."

"It's okay. I'm not blaming you. When you say the body is unrecognisable... what do you mean?"

"I would suggest we don't tell you that at present, just in case it's not her."

"I can't understand your logic. You obviously think it might be her otherwise you wouldn't be here speaking to me, would you?"

He smiled. "We're working through the process of elimination. Any help you can give us to ensure that happens smoothly will always be appreciated."

"My daughter… you're telling me she might be dead, though."

"I'm aware of that. Sometimes the truth is hard to handle." He winced internally at the harshness behind his words. *I really hate this job at times! There was no easy way to inform her. I wish she'd stop asking questions I don't have the answers to.*

She stared at him until Julie cleared her throat and intervened. "It's far too easy to speculate at the moment. We're trying not to get you too involved in the crime, just in case it's not your daughter."

"But the fact you can't tell if it's her or not… that's what's tearing my insides apart. Can you imagine what hearing those words can do to someone? To a parent who has just been told her daughter has been reported missing?"

Julie nodded. "We can. It's a very difficult process we have to work through in order to get to the truth. The facts. Why don't we leave it there for now? We'll contact the dentist and get the information over to the pathologist."

"What then? How long do I have to sit around wondering if it's my baby at the mortuary, or not?" Mrs Watts wiped her eyes on the sleeve of her uniform, but fresh tears soon replaced the old ones.

"Maybe a few days," Julie admitted.

Hero walked over to the door. "I'm sorry. We need to go now. Will you be all right?"

"I doubt I'll ever be all right again, if it turns out to be her," Mrs Watts snapped. She sighed and apologised, "I'm sorry. I know you're only doing your job. Thank you for coming here in person to tell me. I don't think I could have handled it if you'd told me over the phone."

"You're welcome. I'm sorry we've had to be so vague, it's for the best, believe me." Hero left the room, and Julie caught up with him at the main exit.

"Is something wrong? Did I do something wrong?"

"Leave it until we're in the car." He marched ahead and could hear her trotting behind him, trying to keep up.

"Is it because I interfered with the questioning?" Julie persisted on shouting behind him.

"I said leave it, Shaw. Do as you're told."

Once they were back in the car, Hero turned in his seat and tried to explain what was going on in his head. "Don't think I'm bloody angry at you all the time. If anything, the opposite is true. I had a meltdown back there. I didn't know what to say to her. I thought it would be a simple task, but it was much harder than I anticipated it would be. Maybe it was the surroundings doing my head in. I just struggled to make sense of things and took it out on that poor woman. I was an insensitive bastard."

"Oh, I see. So I did good, stepping in like that? You could have fooled me. It's never easy talking to a relative of a victim, if that's what she is. The problem is, we don't know that yet, do we?"

"So you're telling me I approached it all in the wrong way?"

Julie shrugged. "I really can't say one way or another. If you were struggling, maybe you should have excused yourself, instead of making her feel a darn sight worse."

"Don't sugar-coat things, will you?" he snarled.

She glared at him. "I won't. I thought we were speaking honestly."

He swivelled in his seat, his blood boiling, and drove off without responding.

Julie had the good sense not to push things. He was ashamed of the way he'd spoken to Mrs Watts, it had been uncalled for. He wouldn't blame her in the slightest if the woman put in a complaint against him.

Hero drove to the dentist in town and spoke to the man who owned the practice, explaining why they were there. Mr Simpson proved to be an understanding type of man and agreed to send a recent x-ray he'd taken of Lizzie Watts' teeth to Gerrard as soon as possible. Hero thanked the man and left. Still feeling like shit for acting like an arse, he slid behind the steering wheel and mumbled an apology to his partner.

"It's not me you should be apologising to, it's Mrs Watts. Had I been in her position I would have wiped the floor with you."

"Don't hold back, will you?" He groaned, sensing he was in for another bollocking.

"I won't. People have a right to be treated with empathy and respect if their child has been reported missing and a body has shown up. Maybe you should remember that the next time you have a melt-down, as you call it."

"And maybe you should remember who you're talking to."

"Pulling rank isn't going to help either. You're lucky I don't report you to the DCI after the way you spoke to her."

Hero rolled his eyes. "You're kidding me. I wasn't *that* bad."

"You were, you just can't see it."

"All right, let's end this conversation now before we fall out about it. I thought I was doing the right thing, protecting the woman. If that was a relative of mine sitting in the mortuary, I know I would want to be protected."

"I've no doubt your intentions were good, but maybe you should have engaged your brain before opening your mouth, if that was the case."

"Enough. I've had enough. I've already apologised. I'm not sure what else you expect me to do about it now."

It was Julie's turn to remain quiet and contemplative as he put the car into gear and tackled the heavy traffic back to the station, which only worsened his mood.

Once they arrived, he marched ahead of his partner and tore into his office, slamming the door behind him. He sat at his desk, almost regretting the fact that he no longer had a bottle of whisky hidden in his bottom drawer. It had been years now since he'd given up the demon drink and, on the whole, he felt better for it, until days like today came along. He'd given up alcohol to save his family. Images of Fay and the kids swam through his mind. Maybe his mood reflected the fact that his son was in a bad place at the moment.

Then he did something he swore he would never do—rang the school and asked to speak to the headmaster, Mr Styles. Generally, he preferred to hold conversations, such as he had in mind, in person, that way he could read a lot into what people in authority were telling him by their reactions, but he was pissed off and in need of reprimanding someone. Who better than the person who had been put in charge of supposedly protecting his son?

"Mr Nelson, what a pleasure it is to speak with you after all this time. I seem to remember you missing the last couple of parents' evenings, I was hoping to catch up for a chat with you then."

"I'm an extremely busy man, Mr Styles. Dealing with the worst criminals in Manchester raises problems of its own."

"I can imagine. Anyway, what can I do for you today?"

"Bearing in mind how valuable time is for both of us, I'm going to come straight to the point, if I may?"

"Of course. Fire away!"

Hero noted the friendliness in the man's tone and almost backed down. He took a sip of water from the bottle on his desk, cleared his throat and straightened his shoulders in readiness for the fight ahead. "Let's talk about bullying, shall we?"

"I'm sorry! In what respect? The school has a clear no bullying stance. If you're telling me something has occurred then I'll get on to it straight away. Are you?"

"I'm glad you don't treat it lightly. I'm not sure if you're aware of this or not, but yesterday Louie came home battered black and blue from the hiding he'd received from a group of bullies at your school."

The headmaster groaned. "That's a regrettable situation. Why hasn't Louie come and seen me about the issue?"

"Probably because he's either too scared these thugs will strike again or he's too embarrassed to admit they cornered him and gave him a good hiding. What I want to know is what you intend doing about it?"

"As already stated, we detest any form of bullying. I'll call Louie in and have a chat with him. Listen intently to what he has to say and act upon it."

"That's good to hear, except, Louie specifically asked me not to call you. Is there any way you can keep this conversation between the two of us?"

"I can certainly try. Did your son give you any names of the bullies?"

"No. Not a single one. After dinner last night we went to the park as a family, and there were a group of youths hanging around. Louie became very detached from us, uncomfortable in their presence. Making me think they were the boys in question. I don't want Louie being too scared to leave his home, fearing that he might get pinned up against the wall and throttled by these thugs, or any other morons in the future."

"All I can do is ask Louie outright to give up the names. Without them, I'm sure you can imagine, it is out of my hands. I need proof to combat the bullies, but the victim needs to assist me with a statement of events and put names to these individuals. I'm sure you'll understand how these things work, what with you being a detective inspector. We can't proceed without critical proof or evidence, such as your son admitting he's been bullied in the first place."

"That's the frustrating part. In my capacity as a DI, I wouldn't think twice about hauling their arses in here and reading them the riot act, however, I have enough sense to realise how uncomfortable that would make my son's life at school."

"It's a dilemma for sure. I can call a staff meeting and reiterate the school's policy on bullying, to ensure the staff are aware they need to keep their eyes and ears open at all times. We do have a few new teachers at the school at present, so it wouldn't hurt to go over things with them, ensure they understand the gravity of the situation."

"That would be fantastic. I take it you weren't aware of these particular bullies then?"

"No, all has been very quiet on that front for over a year now. It's not a case of me and my staff taking our eye off the ball, I can assure you."

"I see. I wonder why these kids have picked on Louie then, because of who I am, could that be the reason?"

"That could definitely be the case. I promise you, I'll get to the bottom of it."

"Thank you, that's all I can ask. But please, don't mention to Louie that I have contacted you."

"I won't. You have my word. Leave it with me. I'll get on it as soon as I can."

"Which means?"

"Within the next hour. Just to make it clear, we pride ourselves on having a no tolerance bullying attitude. Most schools in the area are rife with bullies, so I'm led to believe. This is the first case that has come to my attention this year, that's how rare it is by comparison."

"That's great to know. In that case, I'll leave dealing with the issue in your capable hands, Mr Styles."

"It's always a pleasure to speak with you, Inspector. Maybe we can have a proper chat at the parents' evening, which I believe is in the next few weeks."

"I'll get the date from my wife and make a note of it in my diary. If I can make it, you have my word, I will. Thanks for taking my call today. I really appreciate the school's stance on trying to suppress these bullies. We are all aware where bullying can lead to in our society. If schools can nip things in the bud early, it definitely makes our lives easier once the kids leave your care."

"Indeed. It's about instilling the right morals in the children from the outset."

"I agree. Hope to see you soon, and thank you again, Mr Styles, good chatting with you." Hero hung up, relieved the conversation had gone better than expected and hadn't ended up adding to his stress levels.

Feeling in a better mood, he left the office and joined the rest of his team. "Tell me you have some good news."

Jason beckoned him over. "This might interest you, sir."

"What have you got, son?" Hero instantly regretted using the word, which made him sound older than his thirty-five years.

"DS Shaw asked me to check through the CCTV footage from last night in the Hyde Road area, and I've come up with this." Jason pointed at his screen, and Hero peered over his shoulder at the image of a white van.

His pulse raced. "White Van Man again, so the cases are definitely linked. Any reg on the vehicle? Too much to hope for, yes?"

"Unfortunately not, sir. If I fast-forward the footage, we can see the van following this young lady on the left. She crosses the main road here, and the van slows down. That's where we come unstuck as it's nearly a quarter of a mile before the next camera crops up."

"Julie, come take a look at this."

Julie left her seat and joined them, wearing a perplexed expression. Jason replayed the footage.

"Interesting," Julie stated.

"Isn't it?" Hero agreed. "The girl, would you say that's Lizzie Watts?"

"The picture is a little grainy, but yes, I would. Is it the same van?"

"Hard to tell. However, I'm willing to take a punt and say it is. Jason, can you try and track the van and the route it takes? See if it leads out towards the woods where the victim was located. Also, see if you can get a good look at the driver, this is all we've got to go on at the moment. Two murders, one white van and very little else. They're either very fortunate or they're professionals at work. Let's hope they're the former and not the latter, otherwise I foresee a tough road ahead of us."

"Two murders that could very well turn into more," Julie reminded him.

"Good point. Two murders in two days, who's to say this won't turn into a killing spree? Come on guys, we need a break, keep digging."

"Digging into what?" Julie shrugged. "We've got nothing else to go on except for the damned footage, and that's useless without a reg to chase up."

"I'm aware of that, Julie, there's got to be more to it. There's also the fact we believe there are two men involved, one driving the van, the other sitting in the back, ready to grab the girls or, as in the first murder, ready to dump the body."

"There is that, not that it helps us."

Julie's negativity was a reality check for Hero. She was right, but on the other hand, he didn't want his team spiralling down the no-chance-of-solving-this-case route. In his experience, it was always important for him to keep the enthusiasm running throughout the team. He clapped his hands to gee them up. "Come on, let's do this for the victims and their families, chaps. Don't forget the three men from the first case we're dealing with. Any news from that yet, or have we taken our eyes off the ball there?"

"Shit, okay, let me deal with that myself," Julie said. She riffled through her notebook for the names.

"Let me know how you get on."

The rest of the day drew a blank with the second case, although Julie managed to track down two of the three men from the dating site. Hero sent Jason and Foxy out to question the men who both had plausible alibis. There was a time when such days used to be topped off with an after-work drink at the pub, not any more, although he was tempted as saliva and the thought of losing himself in a glass of whisky filled every crevice of his weary body. But he resisted, eventually. He drove past the pub and got home just after six-thirty.

Raised voices reached him once the front door was opened. Sammy came into the hallway to greet him, his head bowed, not his usual joyful self at all.

Hero crouched to say hello. "What is it, boy?"

Sammy whined and buried his head in Hero's shoulder.

"It's okay. Let's go and find out what's going on." He patted Sammy on the head and stood.

Sammy stayed in the same spot while Hero pushed the living room door open to find Fay standing in the middle of the room with Louie, who was now two inches taller than his mother, pointing at her and shouting in her face. The twins were huddled on the sofa, looking petrified.

Hero rushed forward. His son seemed out of control. "Hey, what in God's name is going on here?"

Louie faced him, his eyes narrowed in anger and disgust. "And you! You swore to me that you wouldn't do it. You can't help yourself, can you?"

Hero slapped a hand over his chest. "Excuse me? What the hell are you talking, no, let me rephrase that, what in the hell are you *shouting* about?"

"You, going to the school, when I specifically asked you not to."

"Now wait a minute. First of all, we're the parents in this relationship, not you. Your mother and I know what's best for our children, and that includes you. Whether you like it or not, Louie, and your size doesn't matter here, you're still a child at thirteen, got that?"

Fay grabbed his arm. "Why don't we all calm down and discuss this like adults instead of shouting at each other? Say one word out of place and we're all going to regret it."

"Someone has already spoken out of turn, haven't you, Dad? Go on, admit it."

Fay tugged on Hero's arm and asked, "What did you do?"

"What any concerned father would do."

Fay closed her eyes and let out a whimpering groan. "We agreed not to get involved."

"Thank you, Mother. I was here when that agreement was made and now... I'm a bloody laughing stock at school, and your interference has cost me dearly." Louie jabbed his father in the chest.

"Keep a civil tongue in your head, lad," Hero warned, Louie's jabbing sending him off-balance a little.

"Or what? Are you going to lock me up in a cell overnight? Or thrash the life out of me like most fathers do? Except you're not, are you?"

Fay gasped and clawed at Hero's arm, seemingly sensing his temper rising.

"Not what? Come on, let's have it. Air your grievances, lad, if that's what you need to do for us to get past this nonsense. Can I remind you that you're scaring the life out of your sisters over there, or hadn't that thought occurred to you?"

"No, I'm being selfish for a change." Louie's cheeks were the colour they used to be when he'd laughed himself into a frenzy as a toddler. This was different, though. Now they were enflamed because of rage.

Hero turned to his daughters. "Girls, why don't you go upstairs, let Mummy, Daddy and Louie have a chat?"

The girls flew out of the room and took the agitated Sammy with them.

Hero faced Louie and growled, "Don't ever put your sisters in that situation again, you hear me?"

Louie held his gaze, his fury matching his father's. When Louie didn't answer, Hero took a step closer to his son. "I asked if you understood my statement, at least have the decency to respond."

"I won't."

Hero frowned. "Won't what? Put your sisters in that position again or are you refusing to respond?"

"Hero, please. You're being too hard on him," Fay pleaded.

He faced his wife; hurt swam in her eyes. "I'm sorry, Fay, the lad has to know when he's crossed the line."

"I haven't," Louie was quick to say.

"That's where we disagree. You were in your mother's face when I came in. I'm not sure what warrants that type of behaviour. I admit it's out of character for you, but it has to stop, Louie. You're a teenager now, raging hormones et cetera, but there is no way I'm going to allow you to behave that way with either your mother or your sisters. You saw how petrified Zara and Zoe were, you think that's good, behaving in that manner?"

"No. I apologise for that. You shouldn't have wound me up."

"If I've done anything wrong in your eyes then your grievance is with me and me alone, got that?"

"Yes. I'm sorry, Mum, I didn't mean to intimidate you like that."

Fay touched her son's arm. "You didn't, sweetie, but your father is right, if you want to discuss important issues there's a way of doing it, preferably not in front of the twins. They're too young to understand that conversations get heated. All they see is your anger, and that's what they feared."

"I can't keep apologising. I am angry right now." He turned to look at Hero. "I asked you not to get the school involved and you went against me."

"I rang your headmaster and had a simple chat. Made him aware that he had a bullying issue at school. Any concerned parent would have done the same thing, son."

"Why? Why would you embarrass me in that way, when I specifically asked you not to?"

"It's my role as a parent to watch out for you, son."

"Stop saying that."

"What?"

"Son... because I'm not."

Hero stared at Louie, shocked and appalled by the hurtful remark.

"Louie, how can you say that after all Hero has done for you over the years?" Fay whispered, as shocked as Hero.

"All he's done for me? What, kept me away from my real father?"

"I dispute that," Hero was quick to jump in. "Your *real* father took off long before I came on the scene, you can't lay the blame for that at my door."

"Whatever. You're not my father and you had no right contacting the school today."

"Now wait just a second, young man, as your mother, I asked Hero to contact the school on my behalf, for both of us. And you know the reason behind that?"

"No. Surprise me?" Louie crossed his arms, defiance showing its ugly head.

"Because as a family we care what happens to you. I felt Hero could use his influence as a copper to get these bullies off your back. He either did it through the right channels, going through the school, or he could round the boys up on the street. Tell me, which do you think would go down better with the thugs?"

"Neither. I told you I could handle it. You showed a lack of trust in my abilities, that's what this amounts to."

Fay sighed and shook her head. "You're wrong, Louie. All we've done is show you how much you mean to us, and this is the way you treat Hero? I'm appalled by what you've said today.

Downright appalled. Hero is my husband. He has always bent over backwards to treat you like his son, *always*. Even when the twins came along, his love for you never dwindled. Has he ever treated you differently to them? Let me answer that for you, no, he hasn't, not one iota. I'm shocked that you've cast him aside like this. Without his love and care, Lord knows where we, you and me, would be today." Fay pushed a strand of hair behind her ear and stepped forward, towards her son. "I'll tell you where we would be, probably living in a crummy one-bedroom flat in Salford. Can you imagine what your life would be like then, if that had happened?"

Louie bowed his head in shame. Hero felt proud to have Fay as his wife. They were a team, always had been. He struggled to comprehend why Louie was reacting this way.

"I'm sorry. I didn't think." Louie stepped back and tried to walk out of the room, but Fay caught his arm.

"Oh no you don't. We make a pact to work this all out now, or life won't be worth living around here. I've heard about too many families going to pot once their kids hit adolescence, I refuse to let that happen in this household."

"I don't want to discuss it further. Let me go to my room." He wrenched his arm away, making his mother unsteady in the process.

Hero gripped Fay's shoulders to keep her upright. "Okay, enough of this. We're going around in circles and accomplishing bugger all. Louie, I intervened for one reason only, because I love you as a son, as my eldest child. I'm sorry if that isn't good enough in your eyes, and if you'd prefer me to back away, I will willingly do it."

Louie's head stayed low. He shuffled his feet on the carpet, clearly embarrassed at the position he'd found himself in.

"Well?" Hero said, not wishing the unpleasantness between them all to fester any longer than was necessary.

Louie shrugged and walked out of the room. This time, Fay and Hero were too stunned to try to stop him.

Fay buried herself in Hero's chest and sobbed. His heart broke for his wife, she didn't deserve to be treated this way by the son she had raised when his own father had deserted them. "Why? Why has he turned against you?"

"It's puberty, love. Rising testosterone levels, I suppose. I can't say I went through the same with my dad. I admired him. Took pride in having him as a father. Teaching me the rights and wrongs in this world. Maybe Louie is rebelling against that. At the end of the day, we can't force him to love me as his father. Maybe he's just been pretending all these years to appease us."

"No. I don't believe it. This has to have something to do with those bullies, it has to. *Our* son, yes, I will always regard you as his father, he's always been a gentle soul. Why the sudden change in him?"

"It's hard to figure out for ourselves. He has to be the one to open up to us, love. Maybe we should both take a step back, give him some space for a few days to try and work things out for himself. Be there to support him when he needs us. Stop heaping pressure on him."

"I wasn't aware that we were, Hero. He's my life—sorry, I didn't mean it to sound as selfish as it sounded. I don't want us, as a family, drifting apart because of one minor slip-up."

"A minor faux pas that rests entirely on my shoulders. I thought I was doing the right thing. As it turns out, I've probably made things a thousand times worse for all of us."

She placed her hands on either side of his face and kissed him. "You were being you. The caring man I fell in love with all those years ago. I will never regret the day you walked into my life and saved us. Louie won't either by the time I've finished with him."

"I know that look. My advice would be to leave it for now, love. Let him simmer down and work through what we said here tonight."

"I'll get on with dinner. It's a casserole, I only need to boil the veg. Should be about fifteen minutes, tops."

"Sounds good to me. I'll go upstairs and get changed."

Fay went in one direction and Hero in the other. On tired, aching legs he climbed the stairs. After changing out of his suit and into a casual pair of jeans and a T-shirt, he poked his head into the twins' bedroom. They were sitting on the bed, each girl holding a doll, enacting the argument they had seen between their mother and their brother. His heart went out to them. They looked up and both blushed when they realised he was watching them.

He approached them and eased between them. Looping an arm around each of the twins' shoulders, he whispered, "It's going to be all right. Louie was just letting off steam. Yes, he went about it the wrong way, but as adults, we've sorted it out. There's no need for you to be upset."

"But he said nasty things to Mum," Zoe replied, her bottom lip trembling.

"Did he? I'm sure they were said in the heat of the moment and he didn't mean anything by it, sweetie. All is good between us now. Are you two going to be okay? That's my biggest concern. I don't want my beautiful girls getting upset over something as silly as this."

The twins nodded, and both of them held up a hand to high-five him.

"That's my girls. Dinner won't be long. Why don't you wash your hands and I'll go and check on Louie?"

"Will he be eating with us?" Zara rested her chin on the head of her doll.

"Of course. Why wouldn't he?" Hero wasn't sure if that statement was true or not. Only time would tell. He leaned over and kissed the girls on the top of the head. "You guys know how much I love you, don't you?"

Both girls held their arms fully open.

"Yes, this much. We love you, too, Daddy. More and more every day," Zoe told him.

Speaking to the twins always put a different spin on life. His heart suddenly felt much lighter than it had five minutes earlier mid-battle with Louie. He felt grateful to have the twins. "Get washed up and I'll see you downstairs."

He left the girls, happier than when he'd first joined them, and popped next door to see Louie. He knocked on the door. No answer. He tried the door handle, and it opened. Hero eased into the room to find Louie sitting on his bed, playing a game on his iPad. His son ignored the intrusion and kept his head down, giving the game his full concentration.

"Dinner won't be long…" He stopped short of calling him *son* after the tirade of abuse Louie had unleashed downstairs. That was the first time Hero had ever had to stop and think about what to call Louie, in the ten years or so they had been a family, and it stuck in his throat.

Louie grunted. Hero took a few steps forward and stood beside the bed. He was tempted to remove the iPad from Louie just to gain his attention. Instead, he waited and waited until Louie finally put the gadget down and glanced up at him.

"What? I don't want anything to eat."

"Please, Louie, don't be like this. I made a mistake, it's what adults do from time to time in the eyes of their children." Hero flinched, expecting Louie to retaliate harshly, possibly chastising him for not being his proper dad, but the teenager didn't.

"I don't know what to say. I just want to be left alone. Work this out for myself."

Hero nodded. "I can do that. But I also want you to know that I'm here for you, the way I've always been. I'm sorry if I've spoilt the relationship we once had, that truly wasn't my intention. All I was trying to do was to protect you. Bullies are the scum of this earth and need to be dealt with by the appropriate authorities, meaning the school. If they don't deal with these boys then that's where it leads to trouble later on in life and where I become involved."

"I know but I specifically asked you not to say or do anything and you went against my wishes, that's what hurt the most."

"My intentions were good, but they turned out to be the worst thing possible. I'll always regret that. Putting a wedge between us, well, that was something I never thought would happen, not in my lifetime. Can we not forgive and forget and move on from this? For the sake of keeping our family together?"

Louie shrugged.

Hero sat on the bed, and Louie shrank back as though to be that close to him would cause him to catch something contagious.

Hero tried to ignore the emotions welling up inside. "You know

I've always regarded you as my flesh and blood, there's never been a day since your mother and I met that we haven't put you first."

"Apart from when the twins were born," he mumbled.

"All right, I'll give you that one. Of course, when your sisters were born. I couldn't love you any more than I do, Louie." He placed a hand to his chest. "In here, you're a huge part of this family, *my* family. As far as I know, I don't think I've ever treated the girls differently to you, have I?"

Again, Louie shrugged.

"Well, maybe a little, I don't think we've ever sat and had a special tea with your Action Men, have we?" A tiny curl of Louie's lip told Hero all he needed to know. He was finally breaking down his son's barrier. "We could try it one day, if that's what you want?"

Louie's gaze met his, and he shook his head. "I'd rather not, thanks."

Hero felt triumphant. He'd succeeded in getting Louie to look at him and to respond. No mean feat with a stubborn teenager.

"Will you join us for dinner? It'll mean such a lot to your mum and the girls."

He uncrossed his legs and stood. "What are we waiting for?"

Louie walked out of the room ahead of him. Hero continued to smile, mission accomplished, until they entered the kitchen. Louie immediately walked over to his mum and hugged her. He mumbled an apology, and Fay squeezed him and kissed his cheek.

"We love you, Louie, all of us, just remember that."

"I love you all as well. I'm sorry if I don't show it sometimes."

"Let's eat. I'm starving, I could eat a scabby dog I'm that hungry."

"Daddy!" Zara and Zoe screeched.

Even Sammy whimpered at the remark and wandered across the kitchen and into his bed. Louie rolled his eyes and shook his head then sat next to Hero at the table, in his usual spot.

Dinner was a quiet affair, wholesome food, and now that the tension had eased, all was perfect again in Hero's world, for now.

7

*T*he group of men were on the prowl again. Daz had discounted a number of potential women in his search for the next victim until the slim blonde came into view. Short skirt, low top with a cropped cardigan in lace slung around her shoulders to ward off any prospective evening chill. He sniggered at the way she tottered in her four-inch heels. "Some girls need to learn how to walk properly. Why buy the damned shoes if you can't walk in them?"

"It's all about the image, bro."

Daz cast a sideways glance at his brother. "Yeah, she looks like a whore. If that's the image she was going for, she hit the mark, bang on. You guys ready in the back? We're coming up to a junction now, nothing else on the road. Swoop as soon as I stop. There are no cameras around from what I can see."

"We're always ready for some action, ain't we, Todd?" Barry replied, a wide grin pulling at his features.

"Yeah, we were born ready. She looks well up for it, Daz."

"Yep, that's why I've chosen her. Get ready." Daz drew up a few feet ahead of the girl and turned in his seat to give Barry and Todd the thumbs-up.

Barry slid the side door open and hopped out. The girl screamed until he placed his hand over her mouth and shoved her in the back for Todd to take over. The girl nutted him and put up a fight.

Todd let her go, more concerned about his own injuries.

"What are you playing at? Grab her, tie her up if necessary, you know the drill, guys," Daz shouted from the front.

He drove off, and Barry slid the door shut then pounced on the woman.

"Get off me, you frigging prick. Lay one finger on me and you'll bloody know about it. I'm a black belt in karate."

"Yeah, and I'm an expert in origami, so frigging what, you trollop?" Barry sneered at her and burst out laughing.

The girl charged at him, connecting with his paunch and knocking the wind out of him. "Take that, fucker. Think you're going to get anywhere with me, you're bloody mistaken. I grew up with five brothers and wiped the floor with all of them at one time or another. So fucking bring it on, macho man."

"Mouthy fucking bitch." Barry swiped her around the face, hard enough she landed on her back on the floor of the van. "Don't just sit there gawping, frigging tie her up, moron," Barry shouted at Todd.

Todd leapt into action. Swiftly turned the woman over and bound her hands behind her. It didn't stop her kicking out, though. After jabbing Todd in the shins, she used her legs to lever herself against the floor to stand, then she ran at Barry. Nutting him again on the right temple. Blood trickled down her forehead, and a large lump emerged on his.

"What's going on back there?" Daz shouted. "Mick, get in the back and give them a hand."

Mick unhitched his seat belt and climbed through the seats. He ran at the woman's legs and wrapped his arms around them, his head landing close to her crotch. "Calm down, bitch." He tugged her, and she hit the floor with a thud.

"I refuse to give in. Bring it on, with my hands tied behind my back I'm still a match for you, bastards."

Mick searched the immediate area and picked up the large monkey wrench. Without warning, he lashed out. Bone crunched on impact.

Her jaw twisted out of shape, and she fell to the floor, out cold. He rejoined his brother up front and swiped his hands together.

"Good job, bro. I knew I could rely on you to sort her out. We're going to have fun taming her."

Daz drove along the A6, keeping a keen eye on his surroundings. He pulled up outside a metal farm gate. "Todd, get out and open it."

Todd carried out his instructions, and Daz drove through the gate and crossed the large field. He stopped the van and told the men to work quickly. They took it in turns to rape the girl, condoms in place, and then Daz ordered, "Get her out of the vehicle. Barry, there's some petrol left in the can, take it with you."

The woman was unceremoniously dumped on the ground. She was still out cold from the whack she'd received. Daz withdrew the kitchen knife and got to work, ripping through her clothes and discarding them. Gaining access to her breasts, he sliced off the first one. The girl stirred. He clobbered her again, so hard another bone shattered. Daz didn't care, he raised the knife and sliced off the second breast. Then he handed them both to his brother who was holding out a black sack. "More to add to our collection. We'll drag her over there a bit. I want to watch this bitch burn after the hassle she's given us."

Barry and Todd each took a leg and heaved the woman's body around twenty feet away. Daz joined them and tipped the contents of the can over her body. Mick was the one who lit the match and threw it at her. She went up in flames. They walked back to the van and turned to watch the display. Suddenly screams broke out. The woman fought until the end, kicking out and screaming until the flames consumed her body and snuffed out her final breath.

"Oh God, I feel sick." Todd vomited close to the van's tyres.

The rest of the group laughed and then climbed back into the van.

"You're a fucking wuss, man," Daz chastised.

"I can't help it. It was gross seeing her burn like that and hearing her cry out."

"You should be used to it by now," Daz said. He guided the van back to the gate and drove through it. "Secure the gate."

Barry hopped out of the van and closed the gate, then jumped back in and they drove off.

"I'll never get used to it," Todd grumbled.

"Not going soft on us, are you, Todd?" Daz glared at him in the rear-view mirror.

"No."

"You'd better not be, you know what I'm capable of."

8

*H*ero slept well the night before, after his chat with Louie. He was a couple of miles from the station the following morning, when his mobile rang.

"Sorry to trouble you, DI Nelson," the woman on control said. "Is it possible for you to attend a crime scene out at Wychbold's Farm out on the A6, close to Asda?"

"Of course, what type of crime scene?"

"A suspicious death, sir. Thank you for attending."

"No problem. That's what I'm here for. Whereabouts on the farm am I heading? To the farmhouse?"

"No, sir. The field edging the A6. SOCO and the pathologist are already at the scene."

"Rightio. Putting my foot down now. Do me a favour. Get someone to make my team aware that I'm attending the crime scene and ask my partner, DS Shaw, to join me, if you would?"

"Will do that for you, sir. Thank you."

Hero sighed and flicked the switch to engage his siren. The A6 was on the other side of town, it was going to take him at least fifteen minutes to cover the distance.

He drove there in record time, weaving in and out of the traffic when it was safe for him to do so. After spotting the activity up ahead, he switched off the siren and glided to a halt beside Gerrard's van. The pathologist was in the process of retrieving some equipment from his vehicle.

"Gerrard. What have we got?"

"You're going to need to suit up. It's a messy one. I might be going out on a limb here, but my first appraisal would be that this crime was carried out by the same person or persons as the other two cases you're dealing with."

"Dare I ask how you've come to that conclusion?" He took the suit Gerrard offered him and slipped into it.

"You'll see."

He followed Gerrard to the scene, stopping only to sign the Crime Scene Log. Gerrard led him to the middle of a large field adjacent to the main road. Up ahead, Hero could still see the odd waft of smoke and knew instantly what he was about to be confronted with.

"Jesus, not again," he muttered.

"Aye, afraid so. Another malicious act on a female."

"Have you had a chance to examine her thoroughly yet or not?" He glanced at the sky. Overhead were thick black clouds, no rain as yet, but Hero guessed it to be imminent.

"Haven't had a chance yet. We've been preparing the area for the rain that's reportedly on its way. My guys are dealing with putting the tent up, then we'll make a proper start. All I can tell you at this stage is the victim had her breasts sliced off and was then set alight."

"Was she alive when that happened?"

"Your guess is as good as mine. We're talking about callous behaviour here. I don't know how you're going to stop it."

"Callous or warped? Either way, we're going to need you to give us something more at some point, Gerrard."

"I'm aware of that. I'm doing my best. It's an impossible task to attend the scenes, to perform the PMs and to type up all the necessary paperwork. You know how short-staffed we are."

"Sorry, I'm aware of the pressure you're under, it's the same for us.

But without your input on this investigation, we're not going to get very far, that's a fact."

"I understand. I've asked for assistance, but you know how long that's likely to take. I've requested the guys back at the lab to treat your investigation as a matter of urgency, and they're willing to do it, but without any DNA found at the scene, the likelihood of giving you something useful is at an all-time low."

"Maybe we'll strike lucky with this one."

Gerrard hitched up a shoulder. "We live in hope."

The tent was erected before their eyes and placed over the victim. Hero and Gerrard entered the marquee, and Gerrard crouched beside the corpse. Hero watched him take a few samples and fasten the lids on the pots.

He handed them to Hero to bag up. "Might as well make yourself useful. I'll label them in a moment."

"Gerrard, I think you'd better take a look at this," one of the technicians said, poking his head through the flap of the doorway.

"On my way." He groaned as he rose to his feet and shook out his legs. "Bloody pins and needles again. Must get my circulation checked out by a doctor."

"Always a good idea. You can't afford to have time off, how will the department cope?"

"Exactly. Come on, let's see what all the fuss is about."

They followed the technician to a spot in the field. He pointed just ahead of them.

"Interesting. Might be connected, might not," Gerrard announced.

Hero got closer to the pile of vomit. "Good luck analysing that."

"You'd be surprised what we can obtain, DNA for a start."

Hero smiled at the pathologist. "Let's hope it does have something to do with the investigation then. It might turn out to be the vital piece of the puzzle we're searching for."

"Stranger things have happened. Okay, Mike, get some samples for me."

Gerrard and Hero returned to the victim, and Hero said, "It's horrifying to think what the three victims were subjected to before their deaths. I take it she was raped, like the others?"

"I think we can presume that, although I won't make anything official until I've got her back to the lab."

"Anything else you can tell me at this stage?"

"I don't think so. Someone must have driven her here, so maybe you'll be able to pick something up on the ANPR system or CCTV."

"Possibly. Why here?" Hero scanned the area surrounding them. Nothing but fields could be seen until he noticed a white building, he presumed to be the farmhouse, in the far distance. "Who discovered the body? The farmer?"

"Yes. I told him you'd be wanting a word with him. I got the impression he won't be able to tell you very much, though."

Hero sighed. "Nothing new there. The perp is clever, intelligent enough not to leave any loose ends, except one. Maybe he doesn't realise what can be achieved from a pile of sick."

"I hope so. I'd better get on, my workload is increasing daily. The sooner I get her back to the lab the sooner I'll have some news for you."

"Let's hope we find the damned culprit soon. Three victims are two too many in my opinion. I'll speak to you soon. I don't have to tell you how urgent this is, do I?"

"You're right, you don't."

"Sorry, one last thing. The farmer's name?"

"John Alcott," Gerrard supplied.

Hero smiled and went back to his car. He was about to start the engine when Julie parked alongside him. He wound down his window. "Another gruesome murder. I'm just about to question the farmer, see what he has to say. Do you want to follow me?"

Julie sighed heavily. "Not another one. Yes, okay."

They left the field and took a right, back onto the A6. Hero led the way to the farmhouse he had seen on the horizon. In the large driveway, parked at the front door of the old white house, was a red tractor with a bale of straw attached to the forklift arms.

Hero got out of the car and waited for Julie to join him.

"Did you get called out early?" Julie enquired.

"No. I was close to the station when the call came in. I diverted and asked the girl on control to notify you. Let's see what he has to say."

"Dare I ask who the victim was?"

"Too charred to tell. Gerrard believes it was another woman."

"What the hell is going on? Why is the perp bloody burning the victims? Correction, the first vic wasn't, however she was decapitated, that was bad enough."

"He's upping the ante, he's clearly searching for new ways to kill them, although the last two crimes are very similar at first glance."

"A different MO between the final two and the first one, though. It's all rather puzzling, isn't it?"

"Scary. That's what it is. Hard to conceive that all the crimes have been carried out within days of each other. It sticks in my throat." He knocked on the front door.

A man in his fifties, wearing a waxed jacket and sporting a checked flat cap and wellies, opened the door. "Ah, you must be the police. It's about time. I was getting ready to head off again. Some of us have work to do, you know. Time is a valuable commodity most farmers don't have at their disposal. You'd do well to remember that next time."

"I apologise for our tardiness, Mr Alcott. We only got notified of the crime less than half an hour ago."

The farmer gave Julie a cursory glance and then stared intensely at Hero. "Very well. You're forgiven. What do you need to know? Wait, first I need to see some ID from both of you. Can't be too careful these days."

Both detectives produced their warrant cards.

Mr Alcott studied them and then nodded his acceptance. "Right, they seem okay."

Hero placed his ID back in his pocket and asked, "Is there some-where we can chat, sir?"

"Yes, there is, right here."

"If you insist. Maybe you can tell me what time you found the body, sir?"

"It was around sixish, I believe. Might have been slightly before. I'm not in the habit of clock-watching. I do what's got to be done throughout the day without the need to look at my watch all the time. Most farmers are the same. People think we mostly sit around not doing anything all day. Nothing could be further from the truth, I can assure you."

Oh God! We don't need a full-blown explanation, the facts will do. "Thanks. I have to ask what happened when you found the victim."

Alcott frowned. "In what respect?"

"Did it upset you at all?"

"Of course it bloody did. What type of question is that?"

Hero sensed his partner was thinking the same when he caught her looking at him out of the corner of his eye. "Sorry, perhaps I should make myself clearer. When you discovered the body, did you do anything before you rang the police?"

"Like what?" Alcott pointed at Hero and asked Julie, "Is he always like this?"

Julie smiled. "DI Nelson is simply trying to ascertain what happened, sir, kindly answer his question."

"No. How's that? Short and to the point, not that I have a clue what you're getting at."

"There's method in my madness. At the scene, a SOCO technician found some vomit. I had to ask if you had lost your stomach after being confronted with such a gruesome scene."

"Well, why on earth didn't you just come out and bloody say what you meant in the first place?"

Feeling suitably reprimanded, Hero apologised, "Sorry, maybe I should have."

"Vomit, you say? Maybe the killer did it. Hey, you'll be able to get DNA from it, won't you?"

"That's correct, sir. Did you see anyone hanging around?"

"Don't you think I would have tackled them if I had? Or told the operator when I rang up?"

"That's a no then, I take it?"

"Damned right it's a no. If I'd laid eyes on the screwball who'd done that to another human being, I would have battered them. Disgusting behaviour. Worse than any animal I've known over the years, I can tell you. What do you intend doing about it? That's what I want to know."

"Hopefully, we'll use any evidence we've found at the scene to find the culprit or culprits."

"Culprits, you think there's more than one killer?"

"Possibly. We're investigating other crimes of this nature which have taken place this week."

"What? I haven't seen anything on the news about any other crimes. Why haven't I heard about this?"

"Because we've been too busy chasing the clues, sir. We only tend to hold a press conference when the clues have dried up or we need the public's help in identifying the victim."

Alcott's eyebrows shot up. "In this case, you'll be doing that with this victim then, yes?"

"Maybe, sir. Why?"

"I have an enquiring mind. I got a close look at the body, or corpse, it was none too pretty, and I had problems telling if it was male or female. I've been sitting here, with that image running through my mind, wondering how the heck someone goes about identifying the poor person. It's not like there were any possessions like a handbag lying around, was there?"

"You're very astute, sir."

"I like to think so. Before I inherited the farm from my late grandfather, I had in mind that I wanted to be a copper. I watch all the true crime shows going—when I'm not working twelve to fifteen hours a day, that is. I'm one of those who lies awake all night worrying about this, that and the other. Mostly where the next amount of money is going to come from to buy feed for my cattle. Since Brexit, well, I doubt if you want to know the problems we farmers are now being faced with. Most farmers around these parts are thinking of giving up their farms, too much bureaucracy and pages and pages of paperwork to contend with when we have to transport our animals to market. Absolute nightmare, it is. Shameful to put excess unnecessary hours onto our days, as if they weren't long enough already."

"Sorry to hear about the farm. I think you would have made a great copper."

Alcott tutted. "Far too late in life to change things now. What's done is done. Do you need anything else from me?"

"No, I think you've answered everything we need to know."

"One thing, if you do go on TV, is there any way you can keep my name and this farm out of it? You know, don't mention where the body was found, not exactly."

"I think we can work around that, sir. Thanks for dialling nine-nine-nine. Sorry for the inconvenience this has caused for you."

"All I ask is that you find the sick fucker or fuckers who did this." He shooed them away from the door, stepped out and closed it behind him. Then he trotted over to climb into his tractor and started it up. A puff of smoke filled the air, and he drove off without saying another word.

"Funny man," Julie noted.

"Indeed. Right, let's get our day underway, back at the station."

*H*ero stood at the whiteboard, bringing it up to date with the last victim's details. "I sense we're still a long way off solving these cases, team. That's not a criticism, it's a fact. The latest victim was dumped in a farmer's field in this area here." He'd pinned a map of Manchester on another board alongside him. He circled the three areas where the victims were found. "Anything significant jumping out at anyone?"

The team all shook their heads.

"Only that the areas seem to be within ten miles or thereabouts from the city centre," Jason noted, eventually.

"Hmm... it's not enough. We need more, *much* more. I'm going to chase up the lab, try and get them to push the analysis on the vomit found at the scene. That's going to be the key, I'm sure it is. In the meantime, we need to concentrate our efforts on finding the van with no number plate and trying to put a name to the last victim. She had no ID on her person and she was too far gone for us to note any distinguishing features such as hair colour or anything of that ilk. Horrendous, it was. Do your best for me. For the victims. They're mounting up. I want to put an end to the body count now."

"It would help if we knew the killers' motive," Jason said.

Hero nodded. "We're not likely to learn what that is until we find the bastards. We've got two men so far and a white van, plus three victims now, as well. Still nowhere near enough to form any kind of notion about the cases or victims involved. Why dump the body in an open field and set light to it? Why?"

"Each of the crime scenes has been different, is that intentional?" Julie asked.

"Who knows?" Hero was the first to admit. "I'll leave you to it, I'll be in my office if you need me. And don't forget we need to trace the third man from the dating website. Should keep you all busy for a while."

He stopped off at the vending machine for a coffee and then drifted into his office. Brown envelopes littered his desk. He sifted through them and put the contents in piles of importance. After deciding there was nothing urgent enough needing his immediate attention, he called the lab and spoke to one of the leading techs. "Hi, it's DI Nelson. I was hoping you had some news for me regarding the victim whose body was found in the field earlier today. I appreciate you haven't had long, but it's important we get a DNA match, otherwise I can only see the body count rising."

"I understand your concerns, Inspector. I'll give it my full attention now and get back to you ASAP, how's that?"

"I can't ask for more, thank you."

*W*ithin a few hours, Alan, the technician, rang back. "I've got good news for you."

"Well, it's about time. I'm listening."

"We've found a match on the system to the DNA we discovered. A Todd Ford."

Hero leapt out of his seat. "This is excellent news. You're telling me he's already in the system?"

"That's right, for ABH when he was nineteen, back in twenty-thirteen."

"Brilliant. Can you email me your findings, for my records?"

"Doing it now, and you're welcome."

"Thanks, Alan." Hero ran around his desk and out into the incident room. "Listen up, peeps. Find me all you can on a Todd Ford, he's got a previous record for ABH dating back to twenty-thirteen. I want to know where he lives for a start, then I want him picked up and brought in for questioning. Lance and Jason, I want you to fetch him. I need to bring the DCI up to date."

Fingers tapped on every occupied keyboard. Hero dashed out of the room and up the hallway to DCI Cranwell's office. His PA, Sandra, was standing at the filing cabinet.

She smiled at Hero. "Hello, stranger."

"Hi, Sandra, it hasn't been that long since I dropped by to see you, has it?"

"A few weeks. How's the family?"

"We have a teenager who has reached puberty to deal with, need I say more?"

"Ouch, I remember those days well. My husband and I had more arguments through those years than at any other time in our marriage."

"Damn, don't tell me that."

"You have my sympathies. I take it you're here to see the boss?"

"If he can squeeze me in, if not, I can call back another time."

Sandra smiled and winked. "I'll do my best for you." She knocked on the DCI's door. He bellowed for her to go in. "Sorry to trouble you again, sir. I have DI Nelson here to see you, if it's convenient."

"Oh, I see. It's not, but I'll see him all the same. Send him in."

Hero cringed to the point of almost regretting his decision to be there. However, he was aware how gripey the DCI got when he wasn't kept up to date on a case, a new one at that, which appeared to be gaining momentum swiftly.

"Yes, sir." Sandra stood back from the door and gestured for Hero to enter the room. "DCI Cranwell will see you now, Inspector," she said, keeping things professional in front of the chief.

"Thanks, Sandra." Hero swept past her and into the office.

Cranwell had his head down, studying the paperwork in front of him. Hero crossed the room and waited for him to either look up or give him the permission to sit down.

"What are you waiting for, Nelson? The ice in the Antarctic to melt?"

"No, sir. Sorry, sir." He plonked into the chair and waited another few seconds for Cranwell to speak again. This was customary with them. The chief always trying to show Hero that he did his part in the well-oiled machine that was the Greater Manchester Police Force. It all became boring to Hero long ago.

Finally, Cranwell tidied the papers and slotted them into one of the coloured trays on the small cabinet behind his mahogany desk. "Right, now that's out of the way, you have my full attention. I take it you're here about the new case, or should that be cases now?"

"That's correct, sir. At last, we appear to be getting somewhere. So I thought it would be an ideal opportunity to fill you in on the details before things escalate. You know how frantic my job becomes once we have a suspect in mind."

"I do, just like any other inspector's job around the station."

"Indeed, sir."

"Well, get on with it man, stop dithering."

"Sorry, yes. Over the past week we've been dealing with two cases, gruesome cases where two victims, both women, were abducted, raped and killed."

"Horrendous. You mentioned something about a suspect? Tell me how that has come about, will you?"

"Yes, sir. I was called to a further murder scene this morning on my way into work. Another woman, burned to death, lying in a field on the A6."

Cranwell winced. "Yes, yes, spare me the details, especially at this time of day after Mrs Cranwell treated me to a pub lunch earlier. It's our anniversary today."

"Congratulations, sir. Umm… also at the scene, we found evidence that has since been analysed. It got us the result we've been desperate for, since the first victim was found on Monday."

"Evidence? In the form of what?"

"A patch of vomit."

Cranwell screwed his nose up in distaste. "And they were able to get a suspect from that?"

"That's right. The suspect is in the system, so I suppose that made it easier for them. Anyway, this is the first chance I have of filling you in and telling you what we've been up against this week so far."

"I thought you'd been a bit quiet. I heard on the grapevine there had been a few murders. Thanks for eventually apprising me of the situation. Are you going to pick up the suspect?"

"That's the next step. We have CCTV footage of a white van dumping one of the victims. As far as we could tell, there were at least two men in the vehicle. If we pick this man up for questioning, we're hoping he'll dish the dirt on the other suspects involved."

Cranwell nodded and grunted. "In an ideal world that would be perfect. I wouldn't hold my breath on that one, if I were you."

"Yeah, I know it's a tough task ahead. Anyway, you're all up to date now. At this moment, my team are obtaining all the necessary background information on the suspect at their disposal. We'll be bringing the suspect in shortly for questioning."

"Good. Let me know how that goes. I won't hold you up any longer."

Cranwell dismissed him. Hero took the hint and left the room. He expelled a large breath once he'd closed the door behind him.

"Tough meeting?" Sandra asked quietly, her concern evident.

"Not really. I just hate being in the same room as him. Er, sorry… that came out incorrectly. I'm referring to the unnecessary pressure I put myself under when dealing with my superiors, nothing against DCI Cranwell as such."

"I understand. You're a good man, Inspector. Excellent at your job, you have nothing to fear."

"Thanks for the reassurance, Sandra. I must fly, I have a suspect to find and bring in."

"How exciting. Good luck with your mission, Inspector, and with your challenging teenager."

"We'll get there, Fay and I, but thanks. See you soon."

Hero made his way back to the incident room. He sensed the excitement from the team as soon as he entered the office. "Tell me you've got something on the suspect."

"We have," Julie said.

Hero crossed the room to join her. "What have you got?"

"Along with his record, we've discovered he's a labourer with a building firm and we've also managed to find his address."

"Great job. Have Lance and Jason gone to fetch him?"

"They've gone to his address, whether he'll be there is another matter. I'm in the process of looking into the building firm."

"Keep it low-key for now, until we've managed to locate Todd Ford."

"I'll source all the information I can find and sit on it," Julie confirmed.

Hero sensed the investigation was about to come to a head, at least he hoped that would turn out to be the case. He bought coffees for the team as a celebration and handed them around.

Hero placed a cup on the edge of his partner's desk.

"How did things go with the chief?" Julie asked.

"The same as usual, I guess. We need to find this suspect and quickly, Julie. It's going to make our lives so much easier."

The phone on Julie's desk rang. "Hello, DS Shaw, how can I help?" She put the call on speaker as soon as she realised who was on the other end. "DI Nelson is standing right here. What have you got, Jason?"

"The suspect's car is outside the property. Do you want us to see if he's in or shall we sit tight, keep the property under surveillance for the time being?"

"Give it half an hour, observe any comings or goings. If the suspect leaves the property, swoop and bring him in."

"Got that. We'll be in touch soon, sir."

Julie ended the call. "Sounds promising."

"It does, let's not get too excited about it, not yet."

9

*H*ero received the call from Lance and Jason forty-five minutes later. They had picked up the suspect and were en route back to the station. Hero and Julie had the interview room all prepared and were eager to get on with the interview, bearing in mind it was getting on for five o'clock already.

"Looks like another late night ahead of us, Julie. You'd better pave the way at home. I know Fay won't be too impressed."

"Rob will be fine. I'm sure your wife will understand the urgency behind our extended shift."

"Hopefully Ford will give us what we want from the off and we'll be home before *Coronation Street* airs."

Julie's head shot around, and she gawped at him, horrified.

"What's that look for?"

"You don't watch that, do you?"

"Don't you?" He acted as if he'd been offended by her words.

"Occasionally, or should I say rarely? Either way, it's not really a man's thing, is it? To watch the soaps."

"I have my moments. I much prefer *Hollyoaks* to the prime-time soaps."

Julie stared at him, her mouth hanging open for a few moments. "I'm shocked. I never had you down as a soaps addict."

Hero laughed. "Ever been had, Shaw! Really? You think I'd waste my time watching dross like that?"

The colour crept up her neck and into her cheeks. "I should have known you were winding me up."

The door opened, saving her from any further embarrassment. Jason entered the room accompanied by the suspect in cuffs.

"What do we have here then?" Hero sat back in his chair and folded his arms.

"Todd Ford, sir. He kicked off, tried to make a run for it when we reached the car, hence the need to cuff him."

"Thanks, Jason. We'll keep an eye on him. You can remove the cuffs."

Jason did the honours and motioned for Ford to take a seat. "Behave yourself," he muttered in the suspect's ear, loud enough for all of them to hear.

"We're expecting the duty solicitor, can you show them in when they arrive, Jason?"

"I'll do that, sir." He left the room.

Todd Ford glared at Hero and Julie, as if sizing them up. Hero returned the compliment, and the suspect quickly averted his gaze. The awkward silence was interrupted by a knock on the door.

"Come in," Hero shouted.

Jason pushed the door open and motioned for the duty solicitor, Grace Markell, to enter.

"Thanks. Hello again, DI Nelson. All right if I have a quick word with my client before we start?"

"Of course. We'll leave you to it, Miss Markell."

Hero, Julie and the uniformed officer standing at the rear of the room, all left. They waited outside for five minutes until Miss Markell invited them to rejoin her and her client.

"We're ready to begin." Grace flipped open her legal pad and removed the pen from the clip on the side.

Julie said the verbiage for the recording to commence the interview. Hero studied the suspect. His demeanour was one of either shame or defeat, Hero had trouble defining which. Either way, he didn't get the impression the interview was going to take long.

"Thank you for agreeing to come in today, to help us with our enquiries, Mr Ford. Is it all right if I call you Todd?"

"Whatever," the suspect replied with a shrug. His gaze remained focused on the slight imperfection in the table's surface.

Hero asked his first question, "Todd, can you tell me where you work?"

"I'm a labourer. I go where my boss tells me to go."

"No fixed site at present?"

"Not really, no."

"Okay, who do you work for?"

"Chambers and Sons. Why? What's all this about?" His tone was defensive.

"We're conducting enquiries into a few crimes that have been committed this week. Is there anything you want to share with us?"

"Crimes? Such as?" His gaze met Hero's, defiance resonating therein.

"I'll come to that in a moment or two. Maybe you'd care to tell us how your week has panned out so far?"

"My week? I've laid a patio and built a wall on site, is that what you're talking about?"

"And after work?" Hero pressed, tilting his head.

Todd glanced at his solicitor. She looked up from her notebook and gave a single nod.

Todd faced Hero again, smirked and said, "No comment."

Hero raised an eyebrow. "Are you really going to go down that route?"

"No comment," Todd repeated.

"Okay, the thing is, that track tends to be a slippery road to go down. It points at you wanting to hide something. Is that the case here, Todd?"

The suspect grinned. "No comment."

"Very well. If that's how you want to play it. We're at liberty to keep you in a cell for up to twenty-four hours, which can be extended to thirty-six, possibly extended further still by a magistrate to ninety-six. I have time on my side, how about you?"

Todd's eyes narrowed into tiny slits. He then smirked and said the two dreaded words once more.

Hero ended the interview and instructed the uniformed officer to make Todd comfortable in his cell for the night. "Another interview will take place first thing. In the meantime, we'll be digging into your background. It will also give you the chance to mull over whether you want to change your mind on the 'no comment' stance. Sleep well, Todd."

Once the suspect had left the room, Hero asked the solicitor for her opinion. "Did he give anything up?"

"Now, Inspector, you know I can't divulge what is said between my client and myself. He has a right to reply 'no comment' to any questions you fire at him."

Frustrated, Hero lashed out. "Three bloody women have been raped, murdered, dismembered, and in some cases torched this week, and you're telling me that you advised your client to say 'no comment'. Are you for real?"

"I'm sorry about the victims, I truly am. But my priority remains with my client."

"Enough said. I'll give you a call in the morning, when I get around to interviewing him again."

"Can we not make an appointment now?"

"We could, but there again, I'd hate to mess you around if another murder is committed overnight and I have to attend the scene. You see, that's my priority, the unfortunate victims and getting justice for them and the families who are left behind to mourn their losses. Don't expect me to have any type of sympathy with a suspect we can definitely place at the scene of a murder he probably either committed by himself or was a party to with others. Good day, Miss Markell." He turned on his heel and ascended the stairs. He heard Julie mutter an apology as he walked. He was waiting for her at the top of the stairs and wagged his finger. "Don't ever do that again."

Julie seemed stunned at his aggression and covered her chest with her hand. "Do what? What have I done now?"

"Apologise for me. How dare you? What gives you the right, Shaw?"

"I'm sorry," she said meekly. "Honestly, I think you're in the wrong taking your foul mood out on the solicitor, and now me." She barged through the door to the incident room, leaving Hero contemplating his behaviour and lack of professionalism.

He followed his partner into the room, stood by her desk and mumbled, "I'm sorry."

"It's happening all too often," Julie said, keeping her voice low.

Hero was lost for words. He was all too aware how correct Julie's words were, but that didn't give her the right to reprimand him. At the end of the day, he was still her senior. *Start acting like it then and get a grip, man.* He turned away and addressed the team. "Right, well, as you've already guessed by now, we've just conducted one of the shortest interviews ever, because yes, your assumptions are correct, Ford took the 'no comment' route for his responses. Therefore, I'm hoping you guys have come up with the goods for us to sling at him during our second interview, scheduled for first thing in the morning. Have you?"

"I think, between us, we've found quite a bit, boss," Foxy replied. She gathered a few sheets of paper she'd set aside to emphasise her point.

"I'm all ears, Foxy."

"Okay, he's worked for the Chambers Builders firm for the last nine years after he completed an apprenticeship with Solway Builders. Unfortunately, the owner of the firm died and had to lay off all the staff." Foxy set that piece of paper aside and read from the next sheet. "I looked up the electoral roll and found that, until recently, he shared the property with a Lynette Sampson; her name didn't appear on the latest poll as being registered at the address."

"Can we try and find out where she is?" Hero asked. He perched on the desk behind him and motioned for Foxy to continue.

"I'll see what I can do. We also looked at his previous record. He spent four months in prison. While he was in there, the records show that he formed part of a gang, if you like; there were four of them. The others were, Darren Chambers, Michael Chambers and Barry Morris. I'm in the process of finding out more about the three men now."

"Chambers as in Chambers Builders? I'll leave that with you. At least we appear to be getting somewhere. It's late, I think we should call it a day and pick up where we left off in the morning. Good work, guys. I'm proud of you." His gaze drifted to Julie who raised an eyebrow. "All of you," he added.

The team switched off their computers and headed off for the night. Julie lingered and left the station with Hero. He didn't feel the need to apologise again for his earlier conduct. They descended the stairs in silence, and he grunted a farewell at the car.

On the way home, Hero decided to call his sister, to check in with her. "Hi, sis, how are you?"

"I'm okay. Just finished my shift and pushing a trolley around the supermarket at present. Is there something in particular you need, Hero? Not at the supermarket, I meant, is there a reason behind you ringing me?"

"It's about the arrangements we've made for the weekend. I thought I'd better warn you what to expect."

"Hmm... sounds ominous, go on."

"Promise you won't overreact?"

"How can I do that if you haven't told me what it is yet?"

"Ugh... okay, you've got me on that one. Louie is being bullied at school, and he came home with a black eye a few days ago, I think it was, a lot has happened since then."

"Oh shit! Poor Louie. I hope you wiped the floor with the headmaster?"

"Sort of. The problem lies with me contacting the school. Louie now hates me."

"What? No way. He's an intelligent kid, he knows you'd only inter- fere when you thought it necessary to do so. Have you had a chat with him?"

"Yep, it goes without saying, sis, he's shut down on me. Actually, that's not quite true, his actual words were, 'I had no right going behind his back, contacting the headmaster because I'm not his real dad.'"

Cara gasped. "He didn't? Jesus, I doubt he meant it, Hero. He was probably shocked and lashed out in anger. Damn, poor you."

"I'm okay. I was surprised and appalled to hear it. Never thought he would ever hurl that one at me, not after all these years."

"You're hurting, I can hear it in your voice. Before you say it, I would be, too, in the same situation. So, what's the solution? What's Fay said about it?"

"Fay's been my rock as usual, no problem there. As to what the solution is, I have no idea, we're still trying to work it out between us."

Cara sighed. "How have you left it?"

"We haven't really. I love that boy as if he were my own, I have from day one. I knew he and Fay came as a package and I've never thought twice about it."

"I know that. Seriously, I wouldn't read too much into it. From what I've heard, teenagers tend to throw around hurtful comments now and again, with the aim of keeping their parents in line. You just need to stand firm. If Fay is showing you support throughout this then she obviously thinks you're handling it the right way, bro. I feel for you, though. After all you've done for Louie, to have him fling that remark at you must stick in your throat."

"It does. We'll get around it, I'm sure we will. I thought I'd pre-warn you all the same. I didn't want you turning up and thinking all sorts when you saw the shiner he's sporting."

"Thanks for thinking of me. I hope you guys can work it out. Hey, do you want me to have a word with Louie over the weekend?"

"Nah, I wouldn't bother, he'd probably think I'd come running to you for help. Just be there for him if he chooses to confide in you."

"That goes without saying. Any idea who bashed him?"

"Sort of. We went to the park as a family a few nights ago and saw a group of teenagers down there. Louie's reaction was obvious for all to see. He turned back before the twins had a chance to set foot on any of the equipment."

"Would you recognise any of the teenagers again, if you saw them?"

"No doubt about it. I'll be keeping an eye out in that respect, however, Louie was pretty adamant he didn't want me interfering."

"Catch-twenty-two situation, then?"

"I suppose that's what it amounts to, yes."

"Such an invidious position to find yourself in. I'm so sorry, hon."

"It is what it is. You have enough on your plate, I didn't mean to burden you with our troubles. I just wanted you to be prepared, that's all."

"Ever the considerate one. You'll get through this, as a family. I have every confidence in you."

"Thanks. I hope you're right. No, I know you're right. Given time, we'll probably look back on this time and laugh about it."

"That's the spirit. Keep positive. You guys are great together, and I'm sure when Louie is alone in his bedroom, he sits there thinking what it would have been like if you hadn't taken him and Fay on."

Hero laughed. "I doubt that's true, judging by the hatred emanating from him last night. Also, don't let Fay hear you talk about our relationship like that either."

"Me and my big mouth, eh? I wonder where I get that from."

"You cheeky mare. I'd better let you get on with your shopping. Thanks for listening, Cara."

"I'm always here for you. See you soon. Chin up and just continue being you, Hero. It'll soon sink in what a grave mistake he's made."

"I hope you're right." He ended the call and drove home, unsure what kind of reception he was going to get from Louie.

Sammy was the first to greet him at the door. Hero bent down to pet his cherished dog. The twins were the next to bound into the hallway to welcome him home. The love he had for his daughters made his heart sing. He kissed and cuddled the girls while they twittered on about how exciting their day at school had been. He looked up to find Fay, her arms crossed, leaning her head against the doorframe, wearing a huge smile.

Hero unhitched himself from the twins' clinging clutches and approached his beautiful wife. "How's your day been?"

"Fair, I suppose. It's good to have you home, are you hungry?"

"Always. What have we got?" He craned his neck to peer into the lounge.

Fay pointed upstairs. "He's in his room. I've tried a new recipe out for tonight's dinner, I hope it works out okay."

"Sounds intriguing. I'll nip up to get changed." He winked. She read his meaning that he'd look in on Louie at the same time and nodded.

"Ten minutes. Come on, girls, you can help me lay the table."

Hero went upstairs, and Sammy followed at a gallop. After changing into his leisure wear, Hero tapped on Louie's door. "Hi, Louie, can I come in?"

"If you want." His tone was hard to read.

Tentatively, Hero pushed open the door to find Louie sitting on the bed surrounded by school books. "Doing your homework? Or is that a dumb question?"

Louie glanced up, a glimmer of a smile touching his lips. "Yep. How are you, Dad?"

Hero grinned, relieved the problems with his son were no longer an issue. "I'm okay. Hell of a day as usual. Are you coming down for dinner?"

"Yes. Can I have a chat first?"

"Anytime, you know that, Louie." He resisted the temptation to call him son, and it felt so unnatural to him.

Louie slammed his books shut and dangled his legs over the edge of the bed then invited Hero to sit next to him. "I wanted to apologise for the way I overreacted last night."

Hero slung an arm around his son and kissed the top of his head. "There's no need. I was in the wrong, even though it felt like the right thing to do at the time. No harm done in the end."

"Also…"

Hero's stomach clenched at the solitary word. "Go on?"

"I wondered if you would do me a favour."

"Shoot, you only have to ask. What's on your mind?"

"I want to find my real father."

Hero broke out in a sweat, and his heart raced. "Oh, I see. Of course I will, if I can. We're going to have to run this past your mother, see how she feels about it."

"I know. I was hoping you'd do that for me."

Hero snorted. "Too scared, is that it?"

Louie revealed his white teeth in a wide grin. "You could say that. I need to have a connection with him. Need to find out what he's like. What type of character he is, that sort of thing."

"I understand that. There's also the medical side of things. You'll need to know if he's got any ailments or diseases we should be aware of. In years to come you'll need to know that in case anything surfaces. The first thing a doctor will ask is about your medical history."

"I never thought about that before. Do you think Mum's going to mind?"

"Are we talking honestly here?"

Louie nodded.

"Yes, I think she'd be far happier if you never saw your father again. However, I'm sure every child in your position would want to know what makes their absent parent tick. We'll see what we can do. Just to be upfront with you, I won't be able to look for him through the official channels."

"How come?"

"Because we're not permitted to search for personal details in that way, son." *There, I've said it and it felt good rolling off my tongue again.*

"Ah, that could be a challenge for us then. I just assumed you'd be able to use your team to look for him."

Hero laughed. "Sorry to disappoint you. If I did that, I'd be waving goodbye to my career and the pension I've built up over the years."

"Oh no, I wouldn't want that to happen. You've worked too hard to give that up. Forget I asked, it's all right. Maybe it wasn't meant to be."

"Hey, don't give up before we've even started. We'll have none of that defeatist attitude around here, you hear me?"

Louie saluted. "Yes, sir."

"Can I ask why you want to trace him? Why now?"

Louie shrugged and glanced down at his lap. "I don't know. Maybe it's because of what happened. I know that's a feeble excuse, but it was honestly the first time I've thought about him in years. Maybe I'll regret finding him, if we ever do. I also want to tell you..."

Hero placed an arm around his son's shoulders again. "Go on, speak freely."

"I wanted to tell you that I appreciate everything you've done for Mum and me over the years. I was angry yesterday and lashed out for no reason. I'm sorry. Will you forgive me?"

He squeezed Louie and tutted. "Thanks for the admission, there's really nothing to forgive. You know I love you as if you were my own."

"I know. You're the best dad around. I'm sorry if finding my real father is going to cause a rift between us, I don't want it to."

Then leave well alone. Don't pursue this nonsense. You're only going to cause your mother unnecessary grief. "All is good with me, Louie. I can't imagine what it must be like, not having a parent around. I was lucky enough to be part of one of the best family units ever to walk this earth, I believe. Even though Dad passed away a few years ago, I still miss him terribly. I suppose the ache within me has to be magnified hundred times to reflect what you're going through. At least I know where my father is and that he won't be coming back anytime soon."

"You do understand. You're amazing. It's gnawing at me, until it hurts."

He hugged Louie again, desperate to offer the support he'd need for challenges that lay ahead of him throughout his life. Searching for his father was only the beginning of the stresses involved in life's wondrous journey.

"Dinner's ready. Come and get it," Fay shouted.

"Come on, I'm dying to see what this new recipe is. We'll get you what you need, no matter how long it takes to achieve the results."

"Thanks, Dad. You truly are the best. I'm honoured to be your son."

They left the bedroom and raced each other down the stairs, just like they always had. *Why do kids have to grow up? Why can't they remain cute and happy all the time?*

The smell of the dinner greeted them. Hero's gaze was drawn to the table as he entered the kitchen behind Louie. Sitting in the centre was a large serving dish full of pasta with a red sauce. "It smells divine. What is it?"

Fay beamed at the compliment. "Doh, a pasta bake. I hope it tastes as good as it looks and smells." She picked up the ladle and dished up. "I tweaked the recipe a little, added a few ingredients we all like, and this is the result. Dig in, guys. Let me know what you think."

Hero ate the first mouthful, and the taste exploded in his mouth. "It's delicious. There, that's all you'll be getting out of me until I've emptied my plate."

Louie leaned over and kissed his mother on the cheek. "It's scrummy, Mum. Thank you for looking after us so well."

Hero witnessed the tears bulging in his wife's eyes. "You're welcome. Only doing my job, caring for the ones I love most in this world." She glanced up to find Hero staring at her. Fay inclined her head as if to ask what was going on.

He smiled and continued to eat. Ten minutes later, all plates were empty. Two of them, Louie's and Hero's, had even been licked clean. "You'll have to cook that again. It was a smorgasbord of flavours."

"I'll definitely make it again. It only took ten minutes to cobble together. I'm all for the easy life in the kitchen, especially when it's appreciated by you guys. What did you think, girls?"

"Scrummylicious," they said in unison.

The rest of the evening consisted of Fay putting her feet up while Hero and the girls played with the Lego. Louie disappeared back to his room to complete his homework in peace.

Later that evening, in bed, Hero plucked up the courage to tell Fay about his conversation with Louie. To say she was taken aback by the news would be an understatement.

"Why? After all we've done for him? You've always been his dad. He's never wanted for anything in that department. Why now?"

Hero held her tighter. "He's turning into a man. A man has needs. Different needs. I can understand him wanting to find out his roots. We have to do this, Fay. To ignore his cries for help... well, I think that could turn against us in the end. This way, if we give him what he wants, he can never accuse us of trying to keep his father away from him."

She wriggled and looked up at him. "What if we lose him?"

"We won't. If you reckon his father was a piece of lying scum when you were together, I doubt he'll have changed in the years since you guys were with him. If he's still the same then that's the type of man Louie will witness. We'll continue to be the loving, supportive parents we've always been, and he'll soon be able to tell the difference between us."

"Let him go and see if he comes back, is that what you're suggesting?"

"Exactly. I know I overreacted the other day. I've learned a lot from my stupid behaviour."

"Okay. I'll try and find an old address book I have, it'll have the last place where he was living, at least, I hope. Enough about him. Let me show you how much I love you, Hero Nelson. You truly are one in a million, and we're all lucky to have you in our lives."

He chuckled. "Sounds good to me. Oh, and by the way, for the record, I'm the lucky one."

10

*H*ero slammed his hand on the desk in the interview room. He'd tried the softly, softly approach and was getting nowhere fast with Todd Ford. "Let's go over it one more time, shall we, Todd? We know you were at the final murder scene, your DNA was all over the place. I don't think you have it in you to commit these murders alone, so tell us who your accomplices were."

Todd eyed him suspiciously. Hero could tell by the bags under Ford's eyes that the man hadn't slept much the previous night. He wondered if the other gang members would be singing from the same song sheet if they were sitting here now, in custody, accused of being serial killers. He doubted it. The suspect remained quiet.

His gaze drifted over to the duty solicitor and then back to Todd. "Okay, this is what else we have. We've got CCTV footage of you dumping the first victim at Salford Quays. It's not going to take us long to trace the van. We're aware you and your accomplices removed the number plates. Was that a smart move? Nah, I don't think so, there are other ways of identifying a vehicle. No two vehicles are ever the same on the road, are they?"

Todd's eyebrows knitted together. At least Hero had sparked a modicum of interest in the man. "Bollocks. I'm not telling you anything."

"Very well. If that's the way you want it. I'm going to have to make this official then. I've been in touch with the Crown Prosecution Service, and they've agreed that the DNA evidence found at the third murder scene is enough for me to arrest and charge you with murder. We'll await the post-mortem reports from the first two victims and will lay charges on you re the other crimes as and when we hear from the pathologist. The reports are imminent." The ruddy colour instantly drained from the suspect's cheeks. Hero heaped more pressure on him, sensing Todd was about to cave in. "We're aware you've already spent time in prison on an ABH charge and who you hung around with in there. Are you still in contact with the three men? Are they your accomplices?"

Todd shuffled in his seat, gulped and muttered the two words he'd failed to utter since the interview had begun that morning. "No comment." His head dipped.

"I've heard enough. I always take those two words as a sign of guilt. We'll charge you and get you moved to the remand centre by the end of the day. I hope for your sake your mates appreciate your loyalty, Todd. Personally, I think they'll be sitting in their cosy homes, revelling in the fact they've got away with the murders and that you're about to take the fall for all of them. Still, as long as you're happy with events, that's all that counts."

"No, wait. I…" Todd began and immediately clammed up.

Hero sensed he was teetering on the edge.

"Wait for what? The number nine bus to come along?" His tone was heavy with sarcasm.

Todd glared at him, his expression changing before Hero's eyes. He could tell the turmoil was tearing Todd apart. Hero decided to give the man the silent treatment. That's when the sweat broke out on Todd's forehead, left to his own thoughts about what was right and wrong regarding the scenario.

Eventually, Todd heaved out a sigh and muttered, "If I give them up, I need some kind of immunity."

Hero shook his head. "I can't give it to you, not with what we have on you, your DNA at a murder scene. What I can do, is offer to have a word with the CPS, see if they'll be more lenient with you once the trial date is set. How about that?"

After a long pause, Todd nodded. "Okay, I agree. Jesus, they're going to crucify me for this. We're mates. We've been mates for years."

"Since your time in prison together, is that what you're telling me?"

Todd nodded.

"If I reel off the names we have in mind, all you have to do is tell me if I'm right or wrong and all this could be over within five minutes."

Todd stared at him and chewed on his bottom lip. "Go on then."

Hero's gaze dropped to the file in front of him. He opened the manila folder and said, "Here we go then, we've got Darren Chambers." Every time he mentioned a name, Hero paused and looked up to gauge Todd's reaction, and every single time, the suspect winced. "Michael Chambers. And finally, Barry Morris. How did I do?"

Todd shook his head.

"For the recording, Mr Ford is shaking his head. What are you telling me? No, they're not the correct names? No, you don't have any dealings with these men? Be very careful, Todd, we're aware of where you work, remember."

"Yes, you've got the right names."

Hero slammed the folder shut and motioned for Julie to end the interview. Once the recording had stopped, Hero said, "Thanks, Todd. It's in the hands of the CPS now."

Todd's gaze remained on the table.

Hero nodded at the PC standing at the back of the room. "Mr Ford is ready to return to his cell. I'll inform the custody officer of what has taken place here today, and formal charges will be made against you, Todd. I want to thank you for your cooperation."

"Whatever. My life was over yesterday, when you picked me up. Don't expect the others to go down without a fight, just warning you."

"Thanks for the heads-up, I'll take your warning on board."

Hero walked the duty solicitor, Miss Markel, back to the entrance and thanked her for attending. "Thank you for ensuring your client was open with us today."

"All I did was support his willingness to help you. Maybe the spell in a cell overnight was enough to change his mind."

Hero smiled. "It's a great ploy of ours. Thank you anyway. See you soon, no doubt."

"You can pretty much guarantee it, Inspector. Enjoy the rest of your day. I hope it proves fruitful for you."

"Me, too." Hero turned and ran back up the stairs. Julie had already brought the team up to date, so there was no need for him to go over things again. "Right, guys, excellent work so far, but I fear our job is only just beginning."

Foxy raised a hand. He nodded for her to say something. "I've been checking the wires this morning, sir, in case another incident reared its head in line with what we're already investigating, and something caught my eye."

Hero took five paces and stopped at the edge of her desk. "What's that, Foxy?"

"A SOCO team have been asked to attend a site where recent work has been carried out. Apparently, there was an issue with a blocked drain, I believe. Once the site was properly inspected, they found the cause of the blockage, boss—it turned out to be the body of a woman."

"Heck. Find out who's in charge of the case, I'd like a word with them ASAP."

"I'll do it now, boss."

"Okay, while Foxy is sorting that out for us, I want the rest of you to find out all you know about the other three suspects. By the end of the day, I want them sitting alongside Ford in the cells. Thankfully, with a man down it seems their after-hours activity would appear to have been kyboshed. Let's hope so, anyway."

He ventured over to the vending machine and bought everyone a coffee. Julie helped him distribute the cups.

"Can you gee up the team now and again?" he asked. "I don't

suppose they'll need it, but just in case. I'll be in my office for the next few hours. Once I've dealt with the usual dross, I intend to chase up Gerrard, make him aware of what's been happening here."

"This body showing up, I'll keep on top of that, if you like? Let the rest of the team delve into the three suspects' backgrounds."

"Good idea. I'll leave it all in your capable hands."

Julie seemed taken aback by the suggestion. He walked away and settled himself behind his desk to tackle the morning's post. After whizzing through the smaller-than-average pile, he got on the phone to Gerrard and apprised him of the situation.

Gerrard let out a long sigh. "So, you're calling me to hound me, is that it?"

"Not at all. I was merely wondering if you had anything for me yet. It's been a few days since the first murder."

"It has? My, I would never have guessed."

"All right, there's no need to be sarcastic. Where do we stand, and have you heard about the incident going on where a body has been discovered this morning?"

"Yes, I'm aware. I passed it on to a colleague. You may ask why, go on, I dare you."

"Why?"

Gerrard sighed. "Because I'm bloody knee-deep in bodies around here and I've got a blasted restless inspector doing my head in wanting results. Is that a good enough reason to defer the case?"

"Ah, yes. In other words, back off, stop pestering you, which will ensure I get the results far quicker, right?"

"The man does have a brain cell left in his head, after all."

"Hey, that's a bit harsh, even for you. Good job we're old friends."

"Which is why I said it. Now bugger off. I'll get in touch once I have anything of interest to share with you, okay?"

"All right. Is there any point in me apologising?"

"Nope, it'll fall on deaf ears."

Gerrard slammed the phone down. Hero completed the extra task of responding to a number of emails he'd been putting off all week and then he rejoined the team. He bumped into Julie at the doorway to his office.

"Sorry, sir. I was on my way to inform you about the latest body they've found."

He shooed her back and then rested his backside on the nearest desk and folded his arms. "I'm listening. I take it, it's interesting news by the expression on your face, Julie. Either that or you have wind."

"Excuse me! I do not. Do you want to hear what I have to say or not?"

Suppressing a giggle, he gestured with his hand for her to continue. "Go on then. Give it to me."

"I had a word with DI Gall, who is overseeing the scene. He gave the information willingly, aware of the investigation we're involved with."

"Get to the point, Julie, before old age sets in."

She rolled her eyes and then scratched the side of her neck. "So, the owner of the property, it's a block of flats, a Mr Bransby, he said that he'd recently renovated the place and was surprised the body showed up after all the 'damned excavation work' had been completed."

"Hmm… did he say who the builders were who carried out the work?"

"This is where it gets interesting," Julie began.

Hero finished the sentence off for her, "Don't tell me, Chambers Builders were involved."

"All right then, I won't… but they were."

"Jesus! What about the victim? Anything he could tell us there?"

"Only that the body was virtually intact, in other words, decomposition was at a minimum."

"When did the renovations take place?"

"They completed the job last week," Julie confirmed.

"All right. That's yet another nail in their coffins. I think it's time we paid these guys a visit, don't you?"

"I was about to suggest the same."

"Do we know where they're working at present?"

Julie shrugged. "Your guess is as good as mine. Maybe Todd could tell us."

"Yep, we'll ask him on our way out. Gather their addresses for me, and see if anyone has located the vehicle information yet."

"Will do. I'll catch up with you in ten minutes."

Hero raced out of the incident room as DCI Cranwell was reaching the top of the stairs.

"I didn't hear the fire alarm go off, Nelson, what's the rush?"

"The investigation has taken another turn, sir. Sorry, I'm in a hurry, I'll fill you in later." Hero dashed past him, taking the stairs three at a time with his long legs.

"I'll expect a full report from you later today," Cranwell shouted after him.

"You'll get one, sir." He stopped at the reception desk to speak with the desk sergeant. "Ray, I need an extra chat with Todd Ford, in his cell will do."

"I'll get the keys, sir."

Together, they walked the length of the corridor, and Ray opened up the final door. Todd was lying on his bunk, staring at the flaking ceiling. The cells were due to be refurbished later on in the year.

"Todd, I need to ask you what location you're supposed to be working at right now."

Todd remained in the same position. "On a building site."

Hero sighed. "In what location?"

"Salford area. Turnpike Road. There are a few shops at the end, we're ripping the guts out of two of them, making it one large property for a mini-supermarket."

"Great, that helps. Where were you working a few weeks ago?"

Todd refused to answer.

"Todd? Come on, you've been cooperative up until now."

Again, nothing but silence.

Hero glanced at his watch. "I don't have time to hang around. I'll be back to question you further about your recent activity, got that?"

Nothing, again. Hero didn't have the time to push it. He returned to the reception area with Ray as Julie was coming down the stairs. "I've got what we need," Hero told her.

"So have I." She waved her notebook in her hand.

They left the station and hopped in the car.

"What about backup?" Julie was quick to ask.

"We'll see where the land lies first. Credit me with some sense, Shaw."

Out of the corner of his eye, she pulled a face and mimicked what he'd said while wobbling her head. He suppressed the urge to giggle and chose to put his foot down instead, mindful of how she felt about his fast driving. He then gave the air an imaginary strike with his finger and heard Julie huff beside him.

*T*en minutes later, they parked across the road from the shop that was being renovated. Out the front was a plain white van. "Interesting, could be the vehicle used to get rid of the bodies," Hero stated, thoughtfully.

"I'd say that was a definite. What do you propose we do now?" Julie agreed.

"Sit and wait for a while. Let's see what we're up against with these guys. Tell me what you've found out about them."

"Okay, the three men in question are all tradesmen, sorry, two of them are; Michael is an electrician and Barry is a carpenter. While Darren comes under the tag of builder and director of the company. His brother is also named as a director at Companies House. We both know what that means."

"Yep, he takes a share of the company's profits. Anything show up in their personal lives?"

"Something interesting did show up, to me, anyway. The Chambers are twins. They're twenty-six. Darren is expecting a baby with his girl-friend, Trisha Moran."

"What the fuck? And he's going around killing women? What's wrong with the bastards, are they doing this to get their kicks or what?"

Julie shrugged. "Hard to say. All three live with their girlfriends.

Michael's girlfriend is Kim Strange, she works at HSBC in Manchester. And Barry's girlfriend, Stacey, works at the Grey Whistle pub in the city."

Hero nodded, impressed by the information. "Good work. I can't get my head around them all having girlfriends and yet they've been picking up girls off the street, molesting, or should I say raping, them before taking their lives in horrendous ways. How does a bloke even get to that point in his life? Let alone four of them, if you include Ford?"

"Don't ask me. All this is beyond me. They're sick individuals trying to get their kicks out of life, maybe."

"Seems a pretty pathetic motive to me. Hold up, what's going on here?"

The three men left the building site together. They appeared to be animated, as if angry at each other.

"They look furious, all of them," Julie proposed.

"I was thinking the same. Let's follow them, see where they go."

"Maybe they've heard about Todd being in custody."

"That could be the answer, it would be the most logical option."

"Dare I ask if you're going to consider calling for backup yet?" Julie asked, reminding him of procedures he needed to follow.

"Let's leave it for a while, see where they go and make the call at the other end. Don't fret, you're quite safe with me, Shaw."

His partner mumbled something incoherent which he chose to ignore. The van set off, and Hero let a couple of cars go past before he pulled out to follow it. The van gathered speed as it headed into Manchester city centre.

"Backup?" Julie prompted again. "I don't like the thought of us trailing three killers with a couple of pepper sprays and very little else at our disposal."

"Okay, far be it for me to put our lives in danger without the necessary backup in attendance. Organise that for us, if you will?"

His partner didn't need telling twice. Seconds later, she hung up. "I hope they find us before it's too late," she grumbled. She had been unable to give them a location where they were going to end up; after all, they knew very little about the gang's activities, as such.

"Have confidence. We can contact them again further on. Keep your phone handy, not that it's ever out of your grasp anyway."

"This is not the time for sarcasm, boss. I have an uneasy feeling coursing through my veins. Please stay alert at all times."

"That goes without saying, Sergeant, trust me." He continued to follow the other two cars for a while, but the van appeared to be going a lot faster than the others, and it soon became a dot in the distance. *I really must get my sight checked.*

Hero overtook the two vehicles. Julie sucked in a breath. He prepared himself for the barrage of abuse to come. She shocked him by remaining quiet, except for the odd intake of breath and subtle muttering. Now he was behind the van, he really wasn't sure what to do next. Pull it over? Follow it? Drop back a little in case the driver suspected him of being on their tail?

The decision was made for him when the van took a sharp right at the next junction. The fact its tyres squealed told Hero that he'd been spotted.

"Get on that phone of yours, give them our location. Looks like we're heading for the industrial estate, but I could be wrong. It wouldn't be the first time, would it?"

His partner ignored him, she was far too busy making the urgent call. "All done. You think they've got a unit out here?"

"I think we're about to find out. I'm going to slow it down a little."

The van sped up while Hero took his foot off the accelerator. His anxiety gene twitched. *Why do I have a female partner? If I was with another bloke, I'd be going hell for leather, not bothering about the consequences.*

Ahead of them the van took a right. Hero knew the road was a dead end. It consisted of a few large buildings backing onto fields. "This could be it. Get on that phone of yours again, let's keep the backup team updated as much as possible."

Julie did as requested, and then hung up. "Please don't do anything silly."

"I won't. Let's see what the men get up to and then reassess if needed, okay? Trust me, Julie, I've never put you in danger yet, have I?"

"That's debatable. I seem to spend my life on the edge when I'm in a car with you."

He chuckled. "Not what I meant and you know it." He turned right and brought the car to a halt. They spotted the van up ahead, parked at an angle outside one of the warehouses. Hero switched off the engine and reached for the door handle. "You stay here. Wait for backup to locate us. I'm going to take a sneaky peek, see what they're up to in there."

"What if it's a trick? They must have clocked us following them."

"Don't worry, I've got this." He exited the vehicle and darted along what appeared to be a newly created tarmac path.

There was no sign of the three men. Reaching the unit, he eased along the side of the building to a small window. He peered through it and was confronted by several piles of boxes blocking his view. Hero continued on his journey and ended up at the rear of the building. A few feet away he could see a larger window. Constantly aware of his surroundings, he moved closer and looked inside. He spotted one of the men over to the right. He was walking in a circle, pacing, possibly agitated. The other two men were nowhere to be seen.

Again, Hero shifted his position. This time he found himself on the other side of the building. Another couple of windows lay ahead of him. He stopped at the first one and sneaked a peek. The room was dark, possibly an office off the main area. He swiftly moved on to the next window, and when he looked in, the bile rose in his throat. *What the fuck is that? Blood?* It appeared to be a pool of blood, sitting on the floor beneath a chair. *Is this where one of the victims had been killed? Is this a crime scene?* His pulse rate escalated. A sudden noise sounded behind him; he froze in position. Something heavy whacked him on the head. He grunted and nosedived to the ground.

11

*D*istant voices. Head muzzy. *Where am I? What happened? Oh fuck, now I remember. Shit!* Hero inched open an eye and took in his surroundings. He was now inside the building he had been staking out, and the three men were in front of him, arguing about what to do next. He closed his eye again, before they had a chance to spot that he was awake, and listened to their conversation.

"Fuck, man. There's got to be a better way of doing this. He's a copper, for fuck's sake."

"Shut the fuck up! I'm thinking."

"Something you should have frigging done before you knocked him out. We're screwed now."

"What did I tell you?"

Hero heard a thump and a grunt as one of the men hit the floor.

"When I tell you to stay quiet, you frigging do it, got that?"

"All right. Pack it in, you two, we shouldn't be fighting amongst ourselves."

"You got a better idea?"

"No, bro, as you keep telling us, you're the brains of this outfit."

"You're so full of shit, Mick."

"Yeah, always have been, according to you. At least I didn't whack the copper. Fuck it, Daz, you've really hit an all-time low with this one. What are you intending to do with him? Kill him, like the others? The girls? Jesus, how the shitting hell did this get out of hand so quickly?"

"It hasn't got out of hand. All we need to do is kill him and dump his body in the sea. I've got a mate with a boat. It should be a doddle."

"Listen to yourself. You've lost the plot. Read my fucking lips, he's a frigging *copper*! I'm out of here. I ain't doing this no more. You've gone too far this time, bro. I'm through with you."

More scuffling broke out. Hero eased open his right eye again to find one man with his hand around another man's throat.

"Get off me. You're crazy! I want nothing more to do with this shit. Let him go, or we'll all go down for murder."

"Like we ain't going to do that already? We need to get rid of him, and you two are going to help me do it. There's no way I'm going to let you back out now. Get the equipment ready." The one who appeared to be the leader released his hold on the other guy, who staggered a few feet away.

He glared at the leader and shook his head. "I ain't having no part in this, neither is Barry, are you, mate?"

"Nope. I stand with Mick on this one. You're on your own, Daz."

"Okay, whatever. I can do this without you guys, but if I get caught, I ain't going down alone, got that? Here's the thing neither of you have considered. Why do you think a copper is following us in the first place, and where's Todd today? Neither of you could reach him earlier when you tried to call him."

The other two men stared at each other and shrugged.

"Do I have to do all the thinking around here? The police probably picked him up. My guess is from the DNA the tosser left in the field, close to the woman's body. I'm working with damned idiots. The lot of you haven't got it in you to be seasoned criminals, keeping ahead of the police. I need guys I can rely on."

"To do what? Kill more people? You're sick. What's happened to you?" Mick shouted at his brother.

Daz marched towards the other two men. "I'm sick? You two were up for it all the way. Couldn't wait to rape those girls. Yes, I might have killed them, but you were just as much a part of the crime as I was. If I go down, I'll drag you down with me. I reckon Todd has said the same, if the police have already nabbed him."

"We don't know that, you're just assuming that's the case," Mick shouted.

Daz swivelled and walked towards Hero. He closed his eye as soon as Daz turned his way. He felt a jab in his stomach and grunted. His eyes slowly opened to find Daz's face barely six inches from his own.

"Who are you? What do you want from me?"

"Don't give me the fucking innocent act, mate. We know Todd has dropped us in it. Tell me what he's said and I'll go easy on you."

"Todd who? I don't know what you're talking about. I was following a white van that was speeding, next thing I know, I'm here and you have me tied up. What's all this about?"

"That's frigging bullshit, and you know it."

Hero shook his head and winced. "It's not. What's going on, who are you?"

Daz didn't get the chance to answer. In the distance they heard sirens. *Backup is finally here! It's about bloody time!* He groaned.

"Quick, help me get him into the van before they get any closer," Daz said.

"Not a wise decision," Hero advised. "This place will be surrounded in seconds. Give yourselves up and it'll go in your favour when the case gets to court. Flee now, and it's only going to go against you." He looked over at the other two men.

"Daz, he's right. Either let him go or leave him here. We need to get out of here before they pounce and arrest us."

"Chickens. You frigging go. Go on, I don't need you guys any more. I can do this on my own, if I have to. Go on, fuck off." He grabbed Hero by the jacket and yanked him to his feet.

Hero staggered a little, his head still fuzzy, affecting his balance. He was marched through the warehouse and out to the van by Daz. Hero glanced over the road to where Julie was sitting in his car. The door burst open and he shook his head. Julie marched towards them.

"Police. Stop right there!" Julie shouted.

"Shaw, stay back, let them take me. That's an order."

Julie stopped dead and stared at him. "I won't do it, sir."

"Do it. Or I'll demote you." He knew he was talking nonsense, that he didn't have the authority to demote her.

"Backup in the form of an ART is on the way, sir."

Hero cringed. *Why tell them that?* He turned to see the panic rising in the other two men.

"Did you hear that, Daz? You know what ART stands for?" his brother asked, his voice trembling.

"Get in the fucking van, of course I know what it stands for. Put him in the back and tie him up. Keep a close eye on him. We need to get on the road, *now!*"

Hero peered over his shoulder and shook his head, warning his partner not to follow, conscious that he'd left the keys in the damned car. Daz sat up front, and the other two men bundled Hero in the back and bound his arms and legs tightly with thick rope.

"Hey, guys, give me a break, you're cutting off the circulation."

The two men looked at each other and started to loosen the bindings until Daz bellowed, "You dare. Leave them tight. So what if it's affecting his circulation, he won't need to worry about it soon, because he'll be dead. Now stop frigging mollycoddling him."

Daz put his foot down. Every time Hero tried to see in which direction they were heading, Daz deliberately swerved the van, making Hero tumble, often crushing his hands behind him. *Shit! I'm never going to get out of this alive. He's a determined fucker! My only hope is if Julie follows us and leads the ART to the location to attack the bastards. What if they kill me before then? What about Fay and the kids? I can't let Louie down, I've promised him that I'll help him find his father. I will never let the lad down, I can't.* Another dangerous swerve culminated in the squealing of tyres and Hero being thrown to the back of the van.

"Jesus, Daz, slow down, will you?"

Daz let out a demonic laugh. "No intention of doing it, so don't bother asking again. Keep an eye on him. Make sure his hands are secure. You know what the filth are like. He'll be hatching a plan in that tiny mind of his, you can be sure of that. All I'm trying to do is prevent him from doing that by giving him something else to think about." He expelled yet another fiendish laugh.

Hero observed the reactions of the other two men. He could tell they weren't happy and wondered if they were on the turn. *Will they help me when it comes to the crunch? I have my doubts. Daz appears to have them by the short and curlies, he's also out of control.* He caught a glimpse out of the back window. In the distance, he thought he could make out his car, although he was aware how dodgy his eyesight had become recently. The vehicle following them could be a Sherman tank for all he knew.

The van took a sharp right. He noted that Daz was talking to someone on his mobile; their speed had dropped a little during the process. Hero was able to see they were heading down to the harbour at Salford Quays. The van stopped alongside one of the boats, sending the three men in the back sprawling. Hero was no expert, but he reckoned it was a small boat, although he did recognise a large engine on the back, giving him the impression the vessel would be capable of a fair amount of speed. *Hurry up, backup. If you're going to make your move and at least try and save me, now would be the ideal time... just saying.*

Daz tore open the back doors and grabbed Hero by the arm. He was yanked out of the van and landed in a heap at Daz's feet. Daz kicked him hard in the thigh. Hero cried out, more out of shock than through pain, although the kicking had been hard enough to let Hero know the man didn't care what type of damage he did.

"Get him onto the boat, and be quick about it."

Hero was hoisted to his feet by the men either side of him. He was marched onto the boat. Daz's anxious gaze drifted between the control panel and his mobile, as if he had been sent the instructions on how to start up the boat via text.

Great, the fucker has no idea how to start up the darn thing, let alone drive it.

The boat roared into life. Daz checked his surroundings and motioned for the larger of the two guys to undo the mooring. Task completed, he threw the rope back on the bow and made his way to where Hero had been placed, in the middle of the craft. Had the morons put Hero at the side he would have cast himself overboard by now—at least that way, he might have had a chance of escaping his executioners. He stared at the road, willing his own car to appear in the opening. It didn't. Not for a while. Eventually, Julie came to a halt at the edge of the harbour, but by then, it was too late to gain her attention. His stomach dropped as the realisation dawned on him that he was all alone with little to no hope of getting out of the situation if his partner wasn't aware he was on board the boat. He had to think of a way of gaining her attention before it was too late. *But how? With three guys watching every move I bloody make.*

The boat rounded a bend in the river, and the opportunity was lost. Ordinarily, he would have given up but he had no intention of doing that, not if it meant never seeing his beautiful family again. His mind whirred. He'd bide his time, be patient and seize another potential opening when it arose in the future. For now, he considered the route they were taking. He guessed they would be heading for the River Mersey and the gateway to the Irish Sea. That would be a long enough journey for him to come up with a plan to save his arse, surely.

However, their journey was sure to be quicker with the way Daz was skippering the boat. It wasn't his, he had no reason to be considerate in the way he treated it, and he wasn't. Hero glanced behind him: nothing, no sign of anyone coming to his rescue yet, and he doubted they ever would. If he was going to get out of this situation alive, his escape lay in his own hands. The only problem now was that he was tied up and his hands and feet were both out of action.

Ahead of them were a cluster of smaller boats. Hero could hear the people on board shouting at each other. Hopefully, their shenanigans would slow Daz down long enough for help to arrive.

Daz was seething, and he shouted at the group, "Hey, get out of the fucking way, morons. Some of us have a schedule to stick to."

"Take it easy, man. All's good on the water, it's called chill time once you board a boat, you should know that."

"Not this boat. Now get out of the frigging way and let us pass."

Two of the three boats altered their course, and Daz squeezed past them. The urge to reach out to the occupants on the other boats was immense, but the last thing Hero wanted was to endanger their lives as well as his own. In the end, he remained quiet. Letting yet another golden opportunity slip through his damned fingers. *What now? I sit and wait; another chance is sure to come my way soon. Fingers crossed, except I can't, the bloody rope is too tight to do anything and my circulation is suffering badly.*

The boat sped up again. Hero kept an eye out for backup arriving at different sections along the river. Suddenly, a loud speaker announced, "Stop right there. Police. We've got you surrounded."

The three men searched the area in a blind panic. Hero had spotted an officer in black close to the riverbank. He had a weapon aimed at the cockpit. *Do it, take him out!*

A shot was fired. It hit one of the metal bars surrounding the cockpit area.

"Shit! What the fuck? Grab him. Bring him here. Get a move on. You want us all to get shot?" Daz ordered, panic reverberating in his tone.

The two men pounced on Hero and dragged him towards the cockpit as another shot rang out. Hero instinctively ducked. One of the men took the bullet in the arm. *Shit! That was close.*

"What the fuck! Mick, are you all right?" Daz yelled.

"Stop the fucking boat. Surrender or they'll kill us," Mick said, fear resonating in his wide eyes.

"Don't just stand there, Barry, make a tourniquet and put it around the top of his arm before he loses too much blood."

Barry's brow furrowed, and his gaze darted between the two brothers. "A what? What's one of them?"

"Come here. Take over the controls, I'll deal with it."

"No way. I ain't driving no goddamn boat. I wouldn't know where to begin."

"Fuckwit! All you have to do is hold the wheel straight and turn into the bend when one comes up. Do I have to do everything myself?"

Another shot sounded, and this time Barry was struck in the arm.

Not for the first time Hero wished his hands were bloody free. Barry hit the floor, writhing in exaggerated agony until Daz left the controls and gave him a good kicking.

"I'll give you something to scream about, you fucking wuss."

Mick shouted, putting a halt to Barry's punishment. "Daz, the boat, it's going to crash."

Too late. Daz tried to run back to turn the wheel in time, but the front end collided with the bank. He ploughed into the side, hitting his head on a metal railing running around the top of the boat.

"Shit, shit, shit!" his brother shouted.

Barry slid down the deck towards Hero. He came to a halt with a grunt, the wind knocked out of him, beside Hero.

"Free my hands. I can help you all," Hero pleaded.

Barry seemed dazed and confused. He gripped his injured arm and shook his head. "Don't try and trick me. What the fuck do you take me for?"

"You want to get out of this alive? I'm guessing the answer is yes?"

"Of course I do."

"Then undo the rope, free me. I can help you before backup gets here."

Barry's gaze shifted between the two brothers. Mick was at Daz's side, trying to make him more comfortable. "Okay. Give me a tick. My arm hurts like fuck."

"Do you have a knife? You'll need to cut the rope."

Barry produced a flick knife from his pocket and grinned. "I was a Boy Scout in my younger days."

"Great news. Carefully cut through it." Hero turned his back on the man, trusting him to do the right thing.

A few nicks on the wrists seconds later, and he was free. He clenched his fingers closed and released them several times in an attempt to regain the full motion of his hands. It worked. Another shot was fired from the riverbank. Hero ducked and then stood upright and waved his hands. "I'm free. Come get me."

"What the fuck did you do, man?" Mick asked Barry. Daz was beside him, groaning as he regained consciousness.

Hero knew his time was limited. He did the only thing available to him: jumped overboard, into the river. Shouts broke out, more guns were fired. Hero didn't care, he had one course of action on his mind, to get the hell out of there. He swam, his strokes long and strong with determination to save his life.

"Here, give me your hand," a familiar voice said from the bank.

He glanced up and smiled. "Never thought I'd be so happy to see you, Julie."

She helped him climb onto the grass verge. From there, they watched the ART round up Daz and his men.

Hero lay back in the grass, mentally and physically exhausted from his exploits. "Jesus. My life was on the line there, didn't think I was going to make it, not this time. Thanks, partner."

"Are you injured?" She bent down to help him get to his feet.

"No, I don't think so. You drive back to the station, I need to ring Fay."

"Of course. She'll be relieved to know you're safe."

After having a quick chat with the commanding officer of the ART, they got in the car, and Julie drove back to the station.

"Hi, darling. Just a quick call to tell you how much I love you."

"That's unusual. Everything all right, Hero?" Fay asked.

He detected the concern in her tone. "Yes, I'm fine. There's no need for you to be worried, not now."

"What the hell is going on? What do you mean?"

He gave her a brief rundown on what had taken place. She listened, throwing in a few gasps now and then. "Jesus, I'm glad I didn't know about the incident until it was all over."

"As I said, I'm fine. Luckily, I have a change of clothes back at the station. I'll see you later."

"What time?"

"The usual, around six-fifteen to six-thirty. I doubt it will take long to question the suspects."

"Good luck on your mission. And Hero…"

"Yes, Fay."

"Please, no more heroics for the rest of the day."

He laughed. "You have my word on that. Kiss the kids for me."

"I will as soon as I pick them up from school later."

$\mathcal{B}$ack at the station, dried off and dressed in his second suit of the day, Hero walked ahead of Julie on their way to the interview rooms. The three suspects were in separate rooms. Hero's intention was to question all three of them in turn. Using the information gleaned from one of the others. The men were all downhearted, aware of the fate that lay ahead of them. The interviews with Barry and Mick were the easiest. They offered up the information willingly, while Daz tried to fob Hero off by going down the 'no comment' route, just like Todd had tried to do in the beginning.

Eventually, with Hero's skill and patience within the interview room environment, he managed to wear the bastard down. The men ended up admitting to all three murders, actually four—the body found at the building site, Hero had been reliably informed, was that of Lynette Sampson, the former girlfriend of Todd Ford. Her murder had been the catalyst to the killing spree. Todd finally admitted he'd killed her and asked the others to help him dispose of the body. It was Daz who'd come up with the idea of burying her on site. Which meant the gang quickly developed a thirst for taking women's lives, as incredible as that was to believe. Hero felt sick to the stomach by the admission.

Whilst Hero and Julie had conducted the successful interviews, Foxy had arranged for a press conference to take place at five that afternoon. Hero downed a swift cup of coffee then made his way back down the stairs to speak to the assembled press. His aim, to try to obtain the identity of the final victim, the body found in the field. He also announced the arrests of the four killers. Which surprised the journalists who bombarded him with the usual questions, wanting to know the ins and outs of how the arrests were made and, more importantly, what had led Hero to make the arrests in the first place. He gave them snippets of information, details of what he felt they needed and nothing more.

By the time he returned to the incident room, the team had decided between them that Foxy and Jason would work the extra hours needed to cover the phones that evening. "I'm grateful, guys. I'm going to head off home now, I'm exhausted after my adventure today. Please, don't let that prevent you from ringing me as and when anything valuable surfaces, okay?"

Foxy and Jason both nodded their agreement.

"Have a good evening, sir," Foxy said.

Hero bid his team farewell and left the station. The temptation to stop off at his old local was prominent as he drove past, en route to his family. *Boy, could I do with wetting my whistle tonight!*

The children, all three of them, were more excited than usual to see him. Fay shooed them up to their rooms and slipped into his arms. "I'm so glad you're safe. I couldn't imagine my life without you by my side, Mr Nelson."

"I don't intend going anywhere anytime soon, love, you have my word on that."

They shared a loving kiss. Hero ended it and smiled down at his wife, the woman who had captured his heart all those years ago, and said, "What's for dinner, I'm famished?"

Fay swiped his arm. "And there was me thinking you were going to say something romantic for a second there."

"Sorry to disappoint," he teased.

"Sweet and sour chicken. The kids have had theirs already."

"How on earth did you manage that?"

"No-brainer, it's one of their favourites, the smell wore them down in the end. Seriously, how are you? Don't tell me how close I came to losing you, I don't want to know."

"I won't. I'm tired but I'm still here, that's the main consideration, correct?"

"Yes. Of course it is."

"Although, I'm still on call. Some of my team have remained behind, they'll be calling me throughout the evening if any information about the latest victim comes their way. Sorry, love."

"Don't be. I'm grateful you delegated for a change, that has to be a first."

"I didn't. They decided between them and packed me off home. They're a smashing group."

He followed the wonderful aroma emanating from the kitchen, and Fay dished up the sweet and sour chicken on a bed of noodles. He ate it with an eager appetite, not caring that the noodles slapped his chin, slathering it with sticky sauce more times than he cared to remember. He felt relieved to be home, with his family. He pushed aside the thought of how the day might have ended if he hadn't kept his wits about him.

EPILOGUE

*H*ero arrived at work in a buoyant mood, having learned that the press conference had achieved good results. All he and the team had to do now was sift through the leads and see if any of them were related to the fourth victim.

The conclusion, a few hours later, was that there were two possibilities: the first was a woman who had been reported missing over two weeks before, and the other was concerning a young woman whose mother had rung the hotline frantic that her daughter had gone missing two days before. Hero felt the second girl was the likely victim, given that the other victims had gone missing one day and their bodies had been found the next. He and Julie had visited the distraught mother and father of Lizzie Watts and obtained the necessary DNA samples from her clothes, her hairbrush and from her dentist.

Hero then brought his DCI up to date on how the investigation had all come together. He received a bollocking for not reporting to Cranwell the evening before, as instructed. Hero tried to tell the chief he was exhausted by what he'd encountered, but Cranwell was having none of it. Instead, he tore into Hero for being reckless and intentionally putting his life on the line without the necessary backup in place.

He then did something out of character for the chief. He sent Hero home, instructing him to take half a day off.

Not wishing to argue with his boss, he arranged for Julie to tie up any loose ends on the case and instructed her to visit Lynette Sampson's family, the victim whose body was found at the building site, to break the news of her death.

Then Hero went home but instead of resting, he and Fay conducted some detective work of their own. They found that Fay's former husband, Dan Jones, was living in Liverpool. Hero took it upon himself to make the call. The conversation had been tetchy between the two men. At first, Dan said he didn't want to know about Louie, but then curiosity got the better of him. In the end, Dan agreed to meet, fulfilling his son's wishes.

That evening, Fay cooked them a special meal, and together, he and Fay shared the news that Louie had been desperate to hear.

"That's cool. Does he want to see me?" Louie asked breathlessly, hope beaming in his eyes.

Hero gauged his son's enthusiasm. *He'd better not let you down, Louie, or he'll have me to deal with. No one hurts my son and gets away with it.*

After they discussed the matter for a further hour, Hero rang Dan back to arrange a rendezvous for the next day.

The meeting was going to take place at Louie's favourite spot, the adventure theme park. The whole family went, including Cara. Fay nudged Hero as they got out of the car and started to walk towards the entrance. Hero turned to face her.

"That's him. Red jacket up ahead."

"Gotcha. Okay, keep that smile pinned on your beautiful face."

Fay fixed a smile into position and, as a family, they approached Dan. To Hero, he seemed an ordinary kind of chap, but he was aware Dan had a dark side, according to what Fay had told him. Maybe he'd changed over the years. Hero was willing to give him the benefit of the doubt, for now.

Louie shuffled his feet as Fay introduced them. Dan held out his hand for Louie to shake. Louie took it, tentatively.

For some reason, Hero's heart seemed to be lodged in his throat. He coughed to reposition it. "We'll leave you to it. Shall we meet back here in three hours?"

At first, Dan looked shocked by the suggestion, but he soon nodded in agreement. He slipped his arm around his son's shoulders, and they headed off. Although Louie bid them all farewell, he failed to look back in their direction.

Hero could tell Fay was upset. He hooked an arm around her waist and guided the rest of his family into the depths of the park they generally called their second home. Cara walked ahead, hand in hand with the twins.

"He'll be all right, sweetheart. Have faith in him to do the right thing." Hero kept his voice low.

"What if we lose him? What if his father can offer him so much more than we can? What then, Hero?"

"He won't. We have love on our side. Louie will never find what we can give him in that respect elsewhere. Let's see how it pans out first before dwelling on the what-ifs and maybes, eh?"

"Okay. I just feel as though a part of me is missing when he's not around."

"I know, sweetheart. He'll come back to us in a few hours." *I just hope he comes back the same boy who left us.* Hero sensed they had testing times ahead of them with Dan back in their lives.

THE END

$\mathcal{T}$hank you for reading book seven in the Hero series, there will be more to come from the team in the near future, I'm sure. In the meantime, maybe you'd like to try another of my edge-of-your-seat thriller series. Grab the first book in the bestselling Justice here, CRUEL JUSTICE

The debut book in the spin-off series can be found here. **Gone in Seconds**

*O*r perhaps you'd prefer to try one of my other police procedural series, the DI Kayli Bright series here, **The Missing Children.**

*O*r maybe you'll enjoy the DI Sally Parker series set in Norfolk, UK. **WRONG PLACE.**

*a*lso, why not try my super successful, police procedural series set in Hereford. Find the first book in the DI Sara Ramsey series here. **No Right To Kill.**

The first book in the gritty HERO series can be found here. **TORN APART**

Thank you for your incredible support.

If you've enjoyed this story please consider leaving a review or possibly telling a friend.

Mel XX

Made in the USA
Monee, IL
21 July 2021